PRINTHOUSE BOOKS PRESENTS

I0675091

"THE BLOODHOUNDS"
Mystery at St. Christopher's Marsh

VIP INK Publishing Group, Inc.
Atlanta. GA.

"THE BLOODHOUNDS"

Mystery at St. Christopher's Marsh
Editor: Cheryl Hinton
Isbn: 978-0-9978-1165-0
Lccn: 2017938189
Published 5/25/2017
A book based on an original screenplay

"THE BLOODHOUNDS"

By STEPHEN R. ALFRED

STORY BY STEPHEN R. ALFRED AND DANNY WILSON

Cover Art by SK7 & Stephen R. Alfred.

This is a work of fiction. All of the characters, organizations, and events portrayed in this novel either are products of the author's imagination or used fictitiously.

"THE BLOODHOUNDS" Mystery at St. Christopher's Marsh

To
THE ORIGINAL BLOODHOUNDS:
*Danny, Lyndon, Ricky, Wendell, Ashley, Lyle, Larry, Lennis,
and Big Luther...*

And

For

Back-a-town...

"THE BLOODHOUNDS"
Mystery at St. Christopher's Marsh

CHARACTERS

JOHNNY - 12 years old; Unofficial leader of The Bloodhounds. Tends to be cool under fire. Johnny always seems to know how to gets things done and how to get out of a mess.

MARK - 12 years old, JOHNNY'S best friend. Very artistically talented, but doesn't do a lot of talking. Mark's art—and actions speak volumes,

BIG ED, JR. - 11and a-half years old, Big Ed, Jr. is "big" for his age. He hasn't grown into his size 12 shoes. He still "plays with toys," and intuitively knows how to break up a tense moment.

DANNY - 12 years old, Will's fraternal twin brother. Danny is the mischievous instigator of the group. While he isn't always good at getting out of trouble, he sure knows how to get into it.

AUSTON - 12 years old. A real hot-head, Auston loves a confrontation. With an axe to grind and something to prove, Auston is always ready to fight—but it has to be *after church…*

WILL - 12 years old, Danny's younger twin by 3 minutes. In birth, and in life, Will has always been behind Danny. Kind and gentle, Will is the calm where Danny's the hurricane.

MR. WILLIE - Late 60's. Owner of the corner store in, "back-a-town." A WWII vet, Willie has seen a lot. He's watched New Orleans transformation from Jim Crow to the present, offers The Bloodhounds insight, wisdom, and "Snickers bars."

MISS VERNA - Late 60's, Mr. Willie's wife, and co-owner of the store. Verna is like "everybody's grammie." You could depend on her to comfort you when you loss and celebrate you when you won. Tireless in her sense of hope, and in finding joy in the everyday struggle.

MADAME MUVALLA - Voodoo priestess extraordinaire, Muvalla runs a shop in the French quarter. A grifter from birth, she can con the stripes off a zebra.

MORRIS - A long-time hoodlum, Morris is always lookin' for the next big score. He has done prison time before and will not let anything get in the way of a big pay-off.

Acknowledgements

There are so many people to whom I owe the utmost gratitude—the kindest of souls have poured into my life at key points, and…if I leave anyone out (the boundaries of this page make this a certainty), please attribute it to my head (and the page), and not my heart.

To my parents, Louis Alfred Jr. and Eloise Richard Alfred—you poured everything you had into your Son. THE BLOODHOUNDS is but one seed of the harvest. I love and miss you both, "Boonie" and "Pookie."

My family, my wife, Wanda, daughter, Arielle, and grandson, Jayden—you are the reason I do all that I do…

To Pamela (Becky & Jordan) and Louis, whose continued love and support have pushed me beyond the limits of what I thought "I" could accomplish.

To my "spiritual parents"—Pastors Lucius and Donna McDowell, for your unending love, guidance, and support as I continue to walk out my purpose.

To Danny Wilson—one conversation about growing up in the 7th Ward, New Orleans, "Back-A-Town" has grown into a novel, a screenplay, and so much more—A Movement!

To the people of New Orleans, those of the 7th Ward in the 1970's, whose spirits live in the pages of this book. The culture: folkways, music, artistry—all have given breadth and depth to this work that could not have been captured in any other way. It is my sincerest hope that the culture described in this book is a flame that no measure of greed, self-interest, or political agendas can extinguish.

To Zon Pickens (Telezon)—you continue to inspire the "spirit of hustle."

To Abby "Abbiekins" Hurt for your initial reading and analysis of my manuscript and your commentary—you gave me hope to press on.

To Zon D'Amour—your timely visit to Atlanta was the final signal that it was, indeed "time"—thank you so much.

To Antwan, Al, Gia, Cheryl Hinton, and the PRINTHOUSE Books family for enabling me to publish BLOODHOUNDS and to make it available to the world.

Finally, thanks to my Lord, my Savior, Jesus Christ, for allowing me to "live life on purpose," the way I was intended to live.

Table of Contents

PROLOGUE...8

CHAPTER 1 18

CHAPTER 2 36

CHAPTER 3 68

CHAPTER 4 106

CHAPTER 5 139

CHAPTER 6 156

CHAPTER 7 187

EPILOGUE 206

PROLOGUE

I

New Orleans, 1966. Tuesday morning was always a pretty "non-descript" sort of day. The late fall weather began to signal a cold front coming into the city. Delivery trucks clumsily made their way down the relatively narrow streets just off Canal Street, deemed the city's business district.

The Whitney Bank, a symbol of stability in the crescent city for over 100 years, stood at the corner of St. Charles and Common. Yet today, three shadowy figures standing just outside its doors, will threatened its stability. As the mysterious men nod to each other, two enter the building, while the third lingers outside.

Just then, an armored car pulls up to the curb. Two armed guards emerge from the rear of the vehicle and enter the bank with empty moneybags. Now inside, the armored car guards walk up to the bank assistant manager, who guides them to the safe, at the rear of the bank. One of the two mysterious men, who entered the bank earlier, begins to maneuver toward a bank teller's window, as the second man moves toward a lone bank security guard.

The thin man, who remained outside makes his way down the bank's service alleyway. He stealthily moves between an assortment of garbage bags and sanitation bins, to a steel enclosure with a cheap retaining clip as its only means of security. A slight grin emerges on his dark, wind-worn, face as he rips the lock off and opens the enclosure, revealing the bank's phone and electrical boxes. As quickly as he ripped the lock off, he cuts both the phone and the electrical wires. Immediately, the power goes off — the thin man, Robber #3 has done his job...

Meanwhile, Robber #1 makes his move on the Assistant Manager of the bank, and the armored car guards. At the same time, Robber#2 makes his move on the unsuspecting security guard. Robber #1 has a flair for the black-and-white movie bank robbers of old, and clearly gives homage to them in his delivery.

"LADIES AND GENTLEMEN, THIS IS A STICK-UP! THIS IS NOT A DRILL! EVERYBODY PUT YOUR HANDS UP!"

Like a boxer in the clinch, Robber #2 jams the muzzle of his pistol sharply into the side of the Security Guard, who has attempted to draw his weapon. Robber #2 whispers intently, "You DON'T wanna do that, bub... No dead hero's got it?" The Security Guard nods his head and reluctantly surrenders his weapon. Robber#1 addresses the bewildered armored car guards.

"Awright fellas, lose the pieces."

He then addresses everyone in a style and tone reminiscent of the gangsters of old,

"NOBODY MOVES; NOBODY GETS HURT and EVERYBODY LEAVES HERE ALIVE! TELLERS, FORGET ABOUT THE SILENT ALARM AND..."

In a nearby office, the bank manager, Mr. Solire, tries to push the phone off the hook — hoping he can call the police. As he tries to dial the first number, Robber #2 can see the fear and apprehension in Solire's face. With his weapon drawn and cocked, Robber #2 screams,

"HEY, HERO! FORGET THE PHONE, THE LINE'S BEEN CUT! GET OUT HERE, NOW!"

Solire comes out from his office. Robber #1 pulls back from the assistant manager, points to the moneybags, engaging the armored car guards like a schoolgirl who just received flowers from a suitor.

"For me?... Aw Ya' shouldn'a...but, this ain't nearly enough...'know what I mean?"

10

His mood turns nasty,
        "GIMME MORE BAGS...FILL 'EM,
        QUICK!"

Robber #1 shuffles to the rear of the bank, near the safe, where he "encourages" the tellers to fill the bags more quickly...piling them hastily into a nearby bin.

Like a hound's nose, in pursuit of a strong scent, Robber #3's snub-nosed Smith & Wesson revolver's pushes its way deep into the armored car driver's right side. Robber #2 watches as the guards finish loading the last of the moneybags into the armored car. Finally, Robber #1 backs his way to the bank entrance, and confidently makes his parting remarks.

        "THANK YOU LADIES AND GENTLEMEN!
        IT'S BEEN GREAT DOIN' BUSINESS WITH
        ALL-A-YA'LL... YOUR COOPERATION IS
        GREATLY APPRECIATED — AND
        REMEMBER, NOBODY LEAVES FOR AT
        LEAST 5 MINUTES...BE GOOD BOYS AND
        GIRLS... SEE'YA... WELL... MAYBE NOT!

His laughter slowly dissipates into the cool morning air. They'd left as swiftly as they'd entered — commandeering the armored car and pulling off, melting into the city's bustling traffic.

The Napoleon St. Wharf area was not known for its aesthetic beauty, nor for its safety. It wasn't the type of place where one would "show up" in broad daylight, let alone in the middle of the night. The strange and temperamental weather that is New Orleans has now produced a low-lying mist which hovers just below the knee. Against this eerie backdrop a dark sedan pulls up to what would appear to be an abandoned warehouse.

Meanwhile, in the manager's office, the three robbers — all sit at a long-retired office table, rejoicing over their newfound wealth. All around them are stacks of 100-dollar bills, 50's, 20's, the money bands, and the bags they once resided in. Amidst their celebration, four mysterious figures enter the room. Their faces are taut and rigid. Robber#1 has one hand on a stack of hundreds, and one hand under the table — cocking his pistol. The air quickly grows as tense as it is stale. The silence is deafening...

Suddenly, the robber's hardened visage slowly melts into a mischievous grin.

"HEEEEY! Where you guys been? — We jus' been enjoyin' your money!"

The room erupts in almost choral laughter as Robber#1 releases his grip on the pistol in his lap. The four dark figures now step into the light. Three of the men are readily recognizable—they are the three armored car guards from the bank robbery! All of them join in a good laugh, until the din of merriment is broken by the sound of gunfire...

As the smoke clears, three bodies lay in various states of death, strewn amongst the bills, bands, and bags like equally lifeless ragdolls. Silently, methodically, the three guards gather up all of the money, returning it to the moneybags. And the four men make their exit.

II

St. Christopher's Marsh: Narrow strips of solid ground interspersed amongst miles of marsh under a seemingly endless canopy of Spanish moss trees and quicksand... Mosquitoes, snakes, and alligators are amongst its normal residents. Man rarely, if ever is its visitor. However, tonight, the marsh and its inhabitants would unwittingly play host to four men on a mission. The guards— Jack, Mike, and Doug, and their accomplice, make their way through the marsh. The fourth man leads the way—the others do not know where they're going... Still they follow his shadowy figure through this veritable "no-man's-land."

"This place gives me the creeps—"

"Shut-up Mike and keep walkin'," said Jack... "We can't have much further to go..."

"...and why can't we just split up the money and go our separate ways now?"

Jack is becoming more annoyed with every step...

"Becuz, you idiot, this cash is way too hot right now... Besides, any cops notice we've skipped town so close after this gig, and the whole scheme's a bust!"

Doug—nervously quiet up to now, chimes in...
"I just wanna go home guys."

Jack wheels around, at the limits of his patience.

"QUIT YER' WHININ' DOUG!

They trudge through the knee-high grasses and endless mud.
Mike, offering his unwelcomed opinion...

"I think we should split the dough and blow..."

He nudges Jack in the ribs and is now whispering— referring to their unknown accomplice.

"...besides, we just did the guys from the bank...what says he won't try to do us?"

Jack confidently retorts,

"He won't get a chance...We'll drop him as soon as we finish droppin' the dough..."

Doug, overhearing Jack's comments, gives cautious warning,

"...guys, I really don't like the sound a-this...he's the only one who knows how to get outta here. So, how do we get back to the highway?"

Jack, ever prepared, attempts to allay the fears of his accomplice,

"I been leavin' a trail...don't you worry..."

The guards stop at a clearing in an even more remote area of the marsh. As their unknown accomplice stops and turns toward them, Jack and Mike draw their pistols.

"Awright, Morris, end-a-the line...drop da piece," says Jack.

The unknown accomplice finally has a name— Morris... He drops his pistol.

Nervously, Doug backs away from them,

"Jack! C'mon man… this ain't necessary!"

"Shut-up Doug!" snaps Mike. "We need ta' do this!"

Jack notices an old shack on short pilings at the end of the clearing. Motioning with his pistol,

"Up there Morris, get movin'."

Now with a clear upper hand, Jack's bravado starts to emerge...

"you always thought you was smart, and I gotta give it to ya', for a spook… ya' pretty smart..."

Morris, ever the cool customer, is vying for his next move. He has another pistol, and intends to use it, but he's waiting…waiting for an opening… waiting for a sign of carelessness… he figures, he has a little time…until then, he'll let Jack do all the talking.

Jack continues...

"…but, ya gotta be honest, you slipped up… I mean, there's three of us here and just one-a-you, and ya' come all the way out here in the middle a nowhere...with three white men? C'mon!"

Doug, as if he's just along for the ride exclaims,

"Wha — What we gotta do this for, Jack?! We can just blow, like Mike said..."

"Doug, quit yer whinin'! You know we can't leave him alive after all this!"

Now fully intent on his purpose, Jack suggests,

"I mean, think about it...who do you think is gonna be lookin' for a jig like you, out here?"

Morris is beginning to have his fill of the banter.

"...you gonna shoot me, or talk me to death?"

Amazed at Morris' cool in the face of certain death, Jack exclaims,

Oh, you got jokes, eh?! ...A funny dead man? Well laugh at this Ni—

His words are permanently interrupted by gunfire...

CHAPTER 1

It was New Orleans, 1976. One section of the 7th Voting Ward was a mostly Black neighborhood known as "Back-a-town" to 7th ward people. The streets were clean, somebody always cut grass, and the people were always friendly. Kids used to play in the streets, or sit around on front porches. Mothers who worked at home, swept their porches and sidewalks, or had their older children do it. It was before a lot of drugs, and murders; …before things went bad — everybody had a daddy, and everybody's daddy had a job…

For as long as I can remember, we have been "boys." Mark, Danny, Will, Auston, Big Ed, Jr., and me used to be "tight!" The 7th ward was a simpler place, in a simpler time… Black people had what the ol' folks used to call "pride" in themselves back then…

"Miss Mae used to sell "huck-a-bucks," or y'all might call 'em "frozen cups," along with pickles and potato chips two houses down… Danny and Will's mama, we used to call her, "Aunt Mona," used to sell pralines for 10 cents — and they were

BIG too! But her peanut butter fudge was good, yeah... And she used to have that around just for us... After we did our homework and ate dinner, our folks would let us hang out by each other's houses, but the main spot for The Bloodhounds was right in front of Danny and Will's house — on the front porch. We'd be there talkin' and playin' around 'til our mama's called us in for the night.

Friday mornings always meant morning assembly at St. Matthew's Parochial School — all of us 'cept for Auston, who went to Jones School. While we walked about two blocks to get to school, Auston had to walk six blocks across the other side of North Miro Street. Because of us always waitin' for Big Ed, Jr. to meet us in front of Danny and Will's, we were always late for assembly, which was in the schoolyard. We'd always cut through the church to make it look like we were at 8 o'clock mass. We could be late for assembly if we were at church, but we still couldn't be late for roll, especially not on *this Friday*.

This Friday was really important, because it was "graduation and transitional exercises." Every spring, before the Eighth grade graduation ceremony, eighth grade students, in their caps and gowns, were lined up in the main yard, along with the rest of the school. Sister Mary Francis, St. Matthews' Principal, ran the school with an iron fist — and an "iron ruler."

"Good morning students..."

"Good morning Sr. Mary Francis..."

"Good morning, 8th grade parents, faculty and staff... Welcome to St. Matthew's Parochial School's Spring Transitional Program. Here at St. Matthews, we take the time to acknowledge the achievements of our graduating class, and the promise of our wonderful 7th graders..."

In the middle of her morning address, Mark was passing a note to Big Ed, Jr., Who passed it down to Will and finally, Danny, who read the note, and fell out laughing to himself.

"8th graders," Sr. Mary Francis continued, "Ahead of you lay the new and invigorating challenges of high school... There you will learn a greater sense of responsibility to yourselves, accountability to others, diligence in your studies, and fulfillment for your success..."

Danny passed the note back through the line, until it finally reached Mark again—it took everything for him to keep from laughing out loud.

"...it is our sincere hope that you will look upon your years at St. Matthews with fondness... understanding that the foundation laid by the faculty and administration is one of love, respect, and a sense of personal accomplishment...eighth graders, take two steps forward..."

Like a military formation, the eighth graders took the two steps forward, then on Sister Mary Francis' command, turned right, and walked out of the schoolyard.

Next, she turned her attention to us — the seventh graders.

"Seventh graders, take two steps forward — take your place as the new eighth grade of St. Matthew's Parochial School."

All of us, Mark, Danny, Will, Auston, Big Ed, Jr., and me — we all took the two steps forward, occupying the space left by the graduating class. We were at the end of the school year, which meant the 8th graders were leaving after graduation... So we were gonna' be the students in charge now!

Mrs. Dupree's math class was always a class we wanted to get out of — not because of the work, but because she was just so *BORING....*
"Johnny, Mark, report to the office please."
We looked at each other, wondering, "What did we do?" Only when Mark started to smile at me did I remember that gettin' called out of Mrs. Dupree's math class could mean only one thing...

Funerals...

Gettin' called out of Mrs. Dupree's math class
meant gettin' out of class early to serve funerals...
Sometimes we would serve the funerals at St.
Matthew's Church, but sometimes we would
have to go out to the funeral home, which meant
a limousine would pick us up from the church
rectory and bring us to the service. One of the
best things about doin' funerals on a school day
(besides getting' to skip class) was that we'd
usually be finished around lunch, so we'd be
showin' off for the girls during lunchtime,
dressed in our cassocks and surplus' while we
dumped the burned incense outside... Mama used
to say, "Nothin' impressed a girl more than a man
with a job." The other thing about school day
funerals was I always got an excuse to see
Marie... Marie Desvigne (DEZ-VEEN) — I used to
love **EVERYTHING** about that girl!

Whether it was sneakin' by her classroom, seein'
her on the schoolyard, or bumpin' into her "by
accident-on-purpose," I had to see Marie. I
remember one time, Mark and I were puttin' out
the incense on the sidewalk after service, and I
was so busy lookin' at Marie, I dropped some of
the incense on the bottom of my cassock and
almost set myself on fire!

"...talk about 'holdin' a torch for somebody,"
Mark said, "Johnny 'bout ta' make himself into a
torch!"

Ma boy Mark wouldn't let me live that one down,
Noooo...

Marie lived outside Back-a-town, outside the
parish, so I only saw her during school... Marie
was in the 7th grade too... Even though she wasn't
from Back-a-town, her Nanain and Parrain were...

"Nanain and Parrain" were patois names for,
"God-mother and God-father." Ol' Mister and
Miss Desvigne were Marie's daddy's uncle and
auntee, *so they were real old...*

Marie was real smart and real cute, so a lot-a-boys
were try'na to "talk to her." — but Ol'Miss
Desvigne — she wasn't havin' it...

One time, Octave Willard tried to go by Miss
Desvigne's house to talk to Marie...

I'll never forget that! Miss Desvigne said, "Boy...
do you know where you are?! What you doin' on
my porch?! Wait a minute... ain't you that 'WILL-
ARD' boy?! Does your mama-n'em know you on
my porch?!"

Before Octave could get a word in edgewise,
before he could get off the block, Miss Desvigne

had run him off the porch, down the street, and threw a milk bottle at him! She almost took that boy's head off!

Some folks used to make a big thing outta where you were from—some still do... But it didn't matter that Marie wasn't from Back-a-town. She was nice and "really" cute and I liked her... All the boys liked her... *But, I knew she liked me*—and that's all that really mattered...

It was only one more school day 'til the end of the school year, and the beginning of summer. On my bedroom wall, I had a calendar with the 31st of May as the "Last Day of School" and June 1st was circled: "Summer Starts." I would lie in my bed that night and daydream about all the things we were gonna do during the summer.

Summer meant hikin' to Scout's Island at City Park and campin' there all weekend. Our scoutmaster, Mr. Brulliere (BROOL-YAY) would teach us about insects—*he used to have cases full of 'em*; cooking; and about how to win competitions like, "capture the flag." Summer meant picnics and hangin' out in Back-a-town 'til the streetlights came on...

Summer also meant swimmin' at Hardin playground...there were gonna always be too many kids in the pool at the same time, so ya' better know how to swim underwater if you expect to make it to the other side...

One day, after leavin' Hardin, we were all walkin' home — me, Mark, Danny, Will, Auston, and Big Ed, Jr.

"...you seen Todd Narcisse?!" said Danny. "He was try'na show off in front Michelle, and Robin, and her lil' sister, and he buss-a-hole in his trunks!"

"AAAAGGH!" screamed Auston. "...yeah, and he had the nerve to try to act all "ward" when we was laughin' at him... I told him, boy you better look like try'na stitch up yo' draws before you try to come in ma face!"

We all broke out again over Todd and his "hole-ee" trunks, when Big Ed Jr., screamed,

"AAAAGGH!"

"Man the joke done passed... you all late, an — "

"...COO-CORN-BREAD!" Ed was real scared...

We all said it... together... real slow...
"COO...CORN...BREAD..."

Coo-Corn Bread, was a wild-eyed, wild haired man dressed in worn-out army fatigues... he wasn't that big, not that tall, but you know you don't have to be big to be dangerous. We never got close enough to see his hands but some people used to say he had "big man's hands," and that he could palm a grown man's face like Dr. J did a basketball.

You'd only hears kids talk about him — grown folks didn't say nothin' but "don't talk to that man," and "stay away from him…"

Coo-Corn Bread was the only man I knew in Back-a-town who didn't have a job. Nobody knew where he lived either— Mr. Willie and Miss Verna always gave him food though.

Even though grown folks didn't say nothin' about him, we put together some of what we knew with some of what we heard…

We stood there, frozen in time and in space. None of us said a thing… "*Silence*"… but it was as though we all knew what each other was thinkin'. Finally, I got up the nerve to break the silence…

"Coo-Corn Bread…"

"That man scares me for real," said Will

Mark chimed in, "People say he's crazy… Always walkin' around in that same ol' tore up army uniform."

I added, "...some say he went crazy while he was fightin' in Viet Nam...

The tense moment was broken by Big Ed, Jr. who was always sayin' somethin' crazy... then lookin' at all of us, like as if we was crazy.

"...yeah, he killed his wife, and even ate his two kids..."

We all looked at Big Ed, Jr. — like he lost his mind...

"What?"He said.

"People used to say that Coo-Corn Bread was declared insane and sent to a mental hospital" Mark declared, "...but then, they say he was able to get out, on some "technicality," and he's been out ever since, just wanderin' around Back-a-town..."

"Can we go to Mr. Willie's now?" Said Ed. "...that man's scary in broad daylight..."

Mr. Willie and Miss Verna's store, the Hardin Corner Grocery Store, was a typical 7th ward 2 story corner house, with the store on the bottom floor and their house on the top floor. At the corner of N. Dorgenois and Allen Street, the store was right across the street from Hardin

Playground, in the heart of back-a town... The store always needed fixin' but it didn't matter — it was *our store.*

Inside, each narrow isle is full of just about anything that you could get from the big grocery stores, like Winn Dixie, or Schwegmann's. But we came for the sweet and the sour stuff, like "Now & Laters", "Sugar Daddy's" "Hot Dill Pickles", "Pig Lips", "Potato chips," "Snickers," and soft drinks, like "Big Shot Pineapple and Root Beers," THAT STUFF WAS GOOD YEAH!

Mr. Willie was in WWII, and was a surveyor and highway engineer. He was kinda' like ev'rybody's grandpaw... He was real nice to us and sometimes even used to give us free stuff... He always had somethin' funny or somethin' real deep for us to think about, and do...he was our teacher outside of school... And we loved his classroom! He would call us by our individual names, but he always gave our team respect, too.

"SAY BLOODHOUNDS?"

"Hey Mr. Willie... Hey Miss Verna..."

Miss Verna, his wife, was always sweet to us, and always sayin' what good boys we were...and makin' us feel good. We would all try to run from her huggin' us, though...

"Heeyyyy boys, Come here 'en give Miss Verna a hug... Ya'll all gettin' so big, and so fine! Y'all know, ya' ain't too old for a whippin, ya' ain't too old for a hug...what'y'all know good?

"We doin' awright Miss Verna...school's almost over!" I said.

"Y'all got your summer already planned out?"

"We gonna go campin' with Mr. Brulliere"

Big Ed, Jr. said, "we goin' swimmin' at Hardin ev'ryday..."

Mark continued, "we goin' to City Park for Michael's birthday party."

"...and we goin' swimmin' at Hardin ev'ryday," added Big Ed, Jr.

"We goin' hikin' to Audubon park..." Will added,

"Yeah, and we goin' to Pontchatrain Beach..."

"...and we goin' swimmin' at Hardin ev'ryday, said Big Ed, Jr.

Like we always do when Ed keeps sayin' things over, and over again, we just look at him—crazy like...

29

"What?" he said.

Mr. Willie joined in the conversation, "well, it sounds like ya'll got it all mapped out huh? Just remember, ya' need time to do some studyin' over the break..."

"AWWWWWW MAAAAAAAN!"

"No, No... Y'all don't be like that... It's too easy for black folks to be left out of the mix these days, 'specially since we got these "civil rights." Now folks try to hide information from ya' since they can't keep you outta their schools no more...When I was in the service, I can remember serving in France, building roads for our troops and supplies. The company was all black, from the lowest rank on up... When we finished that road, hundreds of miles of newly constructed roadway... We got word that the government was sending a camera crew to film what we'd accomplished... When we got ready to come out, thinking we were gonna get filmed, some officers we'd never seen before, white officers, told us, "you niggers need to stay here, 'til were done...a transport truck pulled up, and a whole bunch of white soldiers piled out, and started posing by OUR EQUIPMENT!"
Then, the cameras started rolling...they made it look like those white soldiers had done all that work, when it was US! Black men toiled and sweat to build those roads... just for them to act

like it was them from the beginning, like we didn't exist... Our C/O said the film was, "to send back to the states to boost morale," and, they didn't know if America was "ready to see black soldiers *in that capacity.*"

None of us breathed a word. It was as if time stood still and brought us to a place we'd never been, to see a sight we'd never wanna see—you could hear an ant walkin' it was so quiet.

Mr. Willie continued, "Some folks'll tell lies that everybody else is gonna believe, so you gotta hang on to the truth for yourself! You gotta remember, NO ONE is gonna "give" you anything! Ya' gotta work for it; work hard now, so you can play hard later! NO one can take what you know to be true from you, NO ONE!"

Auston was the first to say anything. "We understand Mr. Willie; we need to get what they got..."

"That's right son, always get what they got... Too many people, black and white, died and got hurt real bad makin' sure kids like you could move forward in this world as equals...not try'na to be better than white folks, nor better than any other black folks..."

Mr. Willie stepped up to me and pointed his big, cigar-sized finger in my chest — it was like a coach getting his team ready for the big game.

"...just strive to be the best YOU, you can be... Nothin' more... And nothin' less... awright Bloodhounds?"

"YEAAAAAAH!!! We all shouted together. We started to buy a bunch of stuff: potato chips, pickles, soft drinks, and candy –talks like that always made us hungry! As we left the store, always huggin' Miss Verna and waving all the way up the block, Mr. Willie Yelled from the front doorway:

"...and Y'all beat 'dem boys from 'cross the way! Y'ALL FROM BACK-A-TOWN!"

We always felt good comin' outta Willie and Verna's place... They always made us feel special...They were good to us, and what they had to say was always "*good for us...*" We would go back to our usual spot, Danny and Will's front porch, sittin' on the stoop and in that swingin' metal sofa-- eatin' and talkin' 'til our mama's called us in for the night... and even though we were gonna have a whole summer ahead of us to have fun... We couldn't wait for the next school year to start... 'cuz school meant new Pro Keds or Chuck Taylor's...but the next day meant more school, and more work for our folks...

Back-a-town folks were workin' folks... "Workin' class people," we used to hear them call themselves... Nobody we knew was on food stamps or welfare... No drugs, no crime... We all had daddies and all our daddy's had jobs...

My daddy, everybody called "Mr. Richard," was an electrician;

Danny and Will's daddy, we used to call "Uncle Stan," was a letter carrier;
Mark and his brother, Michael's daddy, Mr. Phil, was a carpenter... Mark was one of my best friends—still is...Auston's daddy made sidewalks and driveways outta concrete mix...

Big Ed Jr's daddy, Big Ed, Sr., was a roofer. He was a REAL BIG man and about six-five, almost 300 pounds! None of us could figure out how a roof could hold a man that big...

But, just like Mr. Willie said about us, our daddy's worked hard, so they could play hard—with their families. It didn't have to be a special occasion. Our folks would buy a bunch of ribs, burgers, hot dogs and chicken; they would get a few coolers full of ice from the Gentilly Avenue Ice House, and we'd all be at City Park, barbecuing—the best part was fathers and sons playing football. Later on, the grown folks would be playing Pokeno—we had a lot of laughs and a lot more love...

Even though we had fun, it wasn't always laughs either. We got in our share of trouble too... Grown folks had a lot to say about how you should be as a young black boy... They'd say, "Civil rights had made its mark," and we were the "first-generation beneficiaries..." It was made clear that ya' had a purpose to fulfill, and a lot to learn... So grown folks made a point to correct us the best way they knew how...

The Belt...

And our parents weren't the only ones... when Mrs. Dupree picked up one of the notes I handed Mark and he missed the trash can, she sent us to Sister Mary Francis so fast it made our heads swim! The walk from the classroom, across the schoolyard, and then to the administrative building where Sister Mary Francis' office was our *"via de la rosa."* –the way Jesus was forced to carry His cross to His death. It seemed to take forever to get to her office, and we knew, once we got to the end, a crucifixion was gonna take place. Sister Mary Francis, cool, composed, spoke perfect, proper, Standard English—until you made her mad... When she got ready to whip you, her "slightly Irish" accent got real heavy all of a sudden, as she explained how we were so intelligent and came from good parents, so we needed to make sure we represented our families properly. The volume of her voice always faded,

the closer we got to our reckonin'. While the
Roman soldiers had cat-a-nine tails — Sister Mary
Francis had "the iron ruler." Eighteen inches long,
two inches wide, and three quarters of an inch
thick *(I measured it one day when I was in her office!)*,
the iron ruler was the mainstay of St. Matthew's
corporal punishment program. And after you
caught a whippin' from Sister Mary Francis, you
would catch it again later from ya' mama... And
then ya'd get punished and couldn't go outside,
so ya' gotta watch everybody else playin'
outside... then ya'd get a whippin' all over again
from ya' daddy when he got home from work...
And then ya' gotta hear about it from ya' boys on
the street the next day... But we still did our
"stuff" when we thought we could get away with
it...

...like sneakin' across the London Avenue canal
over the drainpipe...

Three kids drowned in that canal in 5 years, and
our parents made it clear-- if they caught us on
that drain pipe, we wouldn't have to worry 'bout
fallin' in and drownin'...they'd Kill us
themselves...

CHAPTER 2

We used to walk down the middle of the Duels street like we owned it — not in a bad way, like we might rob somebody or somethin — *we didn't start mess*, but we could handle up if we needed to. Other boys from other neighborhoods used to come to Back-a-town, just to challenge us in football. That's how we got our name, The Bloodhounds. We never gave up! We were the Bloodhounds, and Bloodhounds from Back-a-town didn't back down...

We especially didn't back down when we had to play Larry Charbonnet and his boys from across the way...they lived on the other side of Broad Street...them *"cross the way"* boys were the "haters" of our day... Larry Charbonnet and His Boys — Randy, Benny, "Lil Caesar," Aubry, and Gerald all knew how to "run their heads" about what they could do and what they were gonna do... I was like, "shut up and play, man!"

"Fat boy..."

"String bean..."

"Ice wagon"

"Self-check"

"I'm a dus' you…"

"You can't dus' ya mama's coffee table…"

"Feck…"

"Roody-Poo"

Every game, every challenge, started with a combination of stare-downs and put-downs. Them "cross-the-way" boys… they couldn't stand "Back-a-town" boys, and didn't mind lettin' *ev'rybody else know*…they'd come *on our street* and challenge us in football…

After the insults, we'd all agree to the rules. It was our own language we came up with it in the 7th ward, and later, we'd find out kids all over the city were doin' close to the same thing…

"Intercept-Serve…"

"One hand or two"

"One, man! Stop playin'"

"Car-side-out"

"Ok,"

"Straight rush…"

"No, ten count..."

"Man, you can't count to five without messin' up!"

"Ya' maw!"

"Shut up man, les' play!"

Both teams would back away from each other in the middle of the street. Since it was touch football, we played in the street; we had to watch out for cars and hittin' the phone lines with the ball and stuff like that. The one with the biggest arm was always the one you had "serve" — *kick off the ball by passin' it...* While I could throw a lil' it was Mark who had the arm... He cut loose, and the ball went so high and so deep, I thought he was gonna put it in the next block...Then Gerald hollered,

"CAR TIME!"

We all stopped runnin' and moved back against the parked cars along Duels' narrow street, just as a car moved past both teams. Just as the traffic cleared and Mark got ready to serve 'em again...

"Danny? Wiiilll? ...come on inside and eat..." Danny and Will's mama, Aunt Mona, had real bad timing... of all of our mamas, she was always the first one to call her kids in for first one thing, then another... and boy, did it drive Danny crazy!

"Awright mama, can we finish this game first?" The answer was always...

"NO!!! You and ya' brother gonna be 'finished' if you don't get your behinds in this house!" Aunt Mona was nice and all, but you knew not to get on her bad side... Danny used to risk it all the time, but Will knew better...

"Awright mama... Fella's we gotta go eat..." Will started to turn toward the house when Larry snapped,

"Yeah, saved by ya mama..." He was always talkin' stuff, try'na rib somebody... But while Will might just let somethin' like that go, Danny wasn't about to do that, no...

"Say boy, you betta' watch ya' mouth foe' you get snuck up in it..."

I had'ta keep Danny from goin' off on Larry, 'cuz Aunt Mona was gonna watch Danny beat Larry first. Then she was gonna beat Danny for lettin' Larry make him mad, *then* she was gonna *beat Will for lettin Danny get in a fight*, then she was gonna call Larry's mama and tell her how her boy started trouble in front her house — then Larry was gonna get beat again by *his mama*…

Larry used to always act like he was ward or somethin' when he thought people were watchin' him. But I always knew what to tell him to shut him down...

"Boy…you KNOW yo' mama would KILL you if she knew you were out here instead' a mindin' your lil' sister Larry, so don't try to act all *'ward'*…" He knew I was right, 'cuz Miss Charbonnet didn't play — she'd half kill that boy, then go sit down, pick up her *Times Picayune-States Item* newspaper, and drink her *Community Coffee and Chicory* with a good heart…

"Okay... Awright..." Larry said. "We gonna finish this game for real — fecks…Y'all meet us at Dillard, tomorrow, 1 o'clock..."

"…and don't be late neither..." said Randy. "…You late, you lose — again..."

Larry tried to rub it in.

"…yeah, you late, or you don't show, you forfeit..."

"…don't worry, we gonna be there, right BLOODHOUNDS?" I knew we were NOT gonna punk out and miss that game – another chance to beat 'dem boys! Larry and his boys headed up Duels street, toward London Avenue and Broad, back across the way.

Our biggest games were the ones we played against them at Dillard. It was bigger than *Tulane vs. LSU*; bigger than *the Saints vs. the Falcons*...it was bigger than *the Super Bowl*...

Mark kept lookin' at his watch. We were gettin' close to game time, but we were missin' two of our best players – Danny and Will.

"They better get here," Mark said. "...we got less than forty-five minutes to get to Dillard, or we forfeit the game."

Auston was nervous. "Maybe we should just play without 'em..."

"...even if we play without 'em, we'll never win" said, Big Ed, Jr.

I wasn't about to let that slide. "WE'LL WIN...they'll show up – Danny and Will always come through..."

Big Ed came back, "But didn't they go somewhere with their mama...*on the bus?* I was startin' to get tired – tired of Ed complainin', tired of losin' to big mouth Larry

41

and his boys, and tired of feelin' like I had to be the one always holdin' everybody else together. "I SAID they'll be here... Five more minutes..." We had to get to Dillard on time, or we'd have to forfeit the game. Each side had a timekeeper... Mark was ours, and Randy was theirs. We needed Danny and Will to match up against Aubry and Benny on their side, but Danny and Will had went somewhere with their mama and they were late — it would take at least 30 minutes to walk to Dillard....

...unless we went across on THE DRAINPIPE.

Ten minutes pass...

"How much more time we gotta wait?"

"Five more minutes..."

"You said five minutes, TEN minutes ago, Johnny!"

Everything fell silent. Ev'rybody was startin' to get a little nervous — I was nervous for other reasons... Yeah, it was New Orleans, and it wasn't summer time yet ...

So, WHY was I sweatin' like it was already summertime?

Or like I had stolen somethin'?

Mark broke the silence and confirmed my fears.

> "...well, we better at least get a head start and
> get across that drainpipe...it's gonna save us
> about a half-an-hour of walkin' all the way
> around…

Everything else Mark said sounded like gibberish.
All I heard was, "Blah, Blah, Blah, Blah, Blah,
Blah, Blah, DRAINPIPE!"

That explained everything — my hands sweatin,'
my head sweatin, that sick feelin' I always got in
the pit of my stomach whenever my mama talked
about KILLIN' ME HERSELF before lettin' me
cross over that canal… OR ANY CANAL over a
DRAINPIPE… All I could muster up was one
word…

> "But…"

> "Johnny, we gotta go," Mark insisted." Danny
> and Will can catch up…"

I didn't wanna look like some "roody poo,"
scared of a 15 foot drop into a canal with pumps
10 feet in diameter that could drag anything
down to its death… so I put on my game face and
said,
"awright bloodhounds, let's go!"

THE LONDON AVENUE CANAL ...AT DUELS
STREET ...

Many boys had lost their lives playing around
this canal and this particular drainpipe. Back-a-
town parents always warned their children to
stay away from it, and my mama was no
different. My boys didn't know it, but I was
always...scared of heights... and this drainpipe
hung over 15 feet above the canal itself! I could
swim just fine in Hardin's pool—they had a
million lifeguards! But this...this was different. If
I fell in, it was too high and too far for anybody to
help me, and NONE OF US were lifeguards!

Up to now, I always had a good excuse as to why
I didn't need to cross the drainpipe. I could
always come up with a better idea, another plan.
But this wouldn't be one of those times. Danny
and Will were late, it would take us too long to go
around the usual way to Dillard's playin' fields,
and we couldn't lose to Larry and his boys by
bein' late... we would be the laughin' stock of
both our neighborhoods! We would look like we
were "fecks" or somethin'—scared of playin'em...
NO! I had to cross over that drainpipe, no matter
what!

No... maybe I could still find another way...
    "Can't we just..."

"No... We gotta get across, NOW!" said Mark and he just broke out across the pipe like it was nothin'.

AUSTON was next.

"He's right, Johnny...we gotta go"
Auston got over even faster than Mark... the more they made it look easy, the more terrified I got... I still put on my game face...

As Big Ed, Jr. prepared to make his move, it seemed as if he was the only one who could tell that I was afraid. But, just like a Bloodhound, he would never let on..."C'mon man, you can do this..."

Just like his daddy did on those rooftops, Big Ed, Jr. walked carefully, arms extended out, balancing across the length of the drainpipe to the other side.

However, like Jackson's statue in the middle of Jackson Square... I was frozen in front of the pipe.

"C'mon Johnny, you can do it!" said Mark.

Auston was a little less encouraging. "Johnny, c'mon, we don't have all day! What's wrong with him?" he snapped.

"Shut up man, you gonna make him more nervous..."

"But why is he nervous?"

Slowly...and I mean SLOWLY, I started to cross on my hands and knees-- trying not to look down. Then, I held onto the pipe and spread my legs around either side so I was sittin' on top of the drainpipe. I held my breath and began to "slide" across the pipe on my hands and on my butt. I don't know how Danny and Will could do it-- standin' up and walkin' real fast...Danny and Will looked like they were runnin' across that thing when they did it...here I was strugglin' like I was scared I was gonna fall in or somethin'.

The other guys started to *"pick up on"* the fact that I wasn't handlin' this as well as they did. Auston said,

"Don't look down, man!"

"Yeah, keep lookin' at us, keep lookin' at us, Johnny...," said Mark.

Did I mention I had a thing about heights?

And a thing about deep, natural bodies of water?

...since I was a lil' kid, I used to see myself drownin' in my dreams... Or fallin' off-a-high building or bridges...

I would see visions of me fallin' into water, gasping for breath, fighting for my life...

...drowning in the canal.

I know some folks would say a canal is not a natural body of water, but if it ain't a four-foot swimmin' pool, or my bath tub...then it's a natural body of water to me...

All I can do is look down... Then, Mark got my attention again.

"C'mon Johnny!"

"We ain't got all day man, get movin'!"

Now that I was sittin' on top of it, I was movin' across, real slow-like...forgettin' all about the game, and how we'd have to forfeit if we didn't make it there on time...

"Johnny! We don't have much more time!"

For whatever reason, Big Ed's words caused me to grow more panicked by the second, and so I stopped mid-way across the pipe.

"WHAT ARE YOU DOIN', MAN?!" Barked Auston.

Like a whisper at first... I almost couldn't get it to come out...

"I...I can't..."

Ed said, "Yes you can Johnny, don't stop now!

"You're half-way here, man!

The more nervous I was, that's the more irate Auston was.

"I don't believe this, first Danny and Will ain't here, and now Johnny..."

Outta nowhere, Mark jumps onto the pipe, and "runs" across to where I was, still frozen in the middle. I still could not move...my legs were locked solid around the drainpipe, and I could not stop lookin' down. I could hear Auston in the distance yellin' at Mark and me... next thing I knew...I could hear Mark, like he was right across from me...

"Lean forward..."

Mark was in front of me in the middle of the drainpipe.

"Johnny, lean forward, with your chest on the pipe...like 'you huggin' it..."

I broke out of my trance, and began to lean forward, doin' just like Mark said.

"Good, that's good..."

Mark maneuvered around me, got in behind me by stepping over the mesh grating wound around the middle section of the pipe. Then he started to guide me across.

"Okay now, move forward... Put your hands over the other side of the screen... Now climb across, just like I did..."

I did just like he said.

"Good! Now, keep on movin' keep slidin' I'm right behind you!"

"I don't know why I'm actin' like Danny and Will are already here... Even if Johnny makes it across, we still two short," said Auston.

As always, Big Ed, Jr. was more optimistic.
"...Not no more..."

Mark and I were almost all the way across the pipe when we looked behind us to see Danny and Will, running from around the corner, gear in hands, toward the drainpipe! I crossed over, then Mark, and we could see Danny, Will, and their dog, Poochie crossin' the street to the edge of the canal. Poochie was always tryina' follow them everywhere they went. It seemed like the only one he kinda' listened to was Will.

"Poochie! Go Home! You know you can't come with us!"

"Forget about the dog, man we gotta go!" said Danny.

Poochie whined in protest, and then backed his way across the street toward home. Mark yelled to Danny and Will to get movin'.

"C'mon, y'all! We got 18 minutes before we gotta forfeit the game!"

Like I said before, Danny and Will could run over those drainpipes like it was runnin' on the sidewalk...we made it to Dillard with 5 minutes to spare, Larry Charbonnet probably thought for sure they was gonna get a easy win...

...but we THE BLOODHOUNDS...

...and <u>we</u> don't give up that easy...

Larry, Randy, and their boys are a bit surprised that The Bloodhounds made it. They figured we weren't gonna make it, but now they knew they would have to actually "play" the game. As usual, Larry began his usual head games. So he says to Randy,

"Well looka' here... They made it!"

Randy looks at his watch,

"...well, they on time..."
"'No matter, they still gon' get they' issue..."
"We here, Larry!" Auston yelled across the field.

"Yeah, I see... But it ain't gonna matter."

"...and Why NOT?!"

"'Cuz..."

"'Cuz what?!"

The back and forth between Larry and Auston was interrupted by a dog growlin'. Poochie, Danny and Will's dog, tracked us all the way to Dillard! To this day, I don't know whether he followed us over the drainpipe, or tracked us some other way. None of us could believe it, Will least of all.

"Poochie?!"

"What, y'all got a mascot too?" said Larry, and his boys all fell out laughin'.

"Oh, you a funny man huh?" said Danny.

Larry was still laughing, "I'm just sayin'..."

Auston got embarrassed and started actin' like it was Will's fault the dog was there.

"What's with this dog, man? I thought y'all told him to go home?"

Big Ed said, "...he tracked us all the way here!"

"BLOODHOUNDS??!" Said LARRY, and his boys all fell out laughin' again.

"Poochie's jus' lookin' out for us," said Will.

Larry always had a comeback.

"Well maybe HE can play some defense!...Look! He growlin' too! What y'all need to do is put that dog on a leash... He's sooooo ferocious..."

The more Larry and his boys laughed, the madder Danny and Will got, the more we wanted to fight rather than play football. Poochie started to move toward Larry and Randy but Will got hold of him by his collar

Randy picked up where Larry left off.

"Man hold ya' dog... I mean, **hold Auston...**"

Everybody knew Auston was a hothead and it didn't take much to make him wanna fight. To say his daddy was a deacon, that boy sure loved to fight! As he started to move toward Randy, Big Ed, Jr. steps in-between 'em, while Mark and me held Auston.

"Boy, I'm gonna..."

"Remember Auston, your fight is not in the flesh..."

Auston looked at Big Ed, as if to say, 'WHAT?!' Just then, Benny, another one of the cross-the-way boys, stirred up the pot.

"What... We workin' you church-boy?!"

I thought Auston was gonna come outta his skin.

"Man jus' let me..."

"Cool it Auston..." I said. "We got a game to win..."

I calmed Auston down, and then turned my sights on Larry. He and I met up at the mid-field. Normally, teams flipped coins and shook hands.

Not us...

"You "fecks" gonna get it today, 'cuz we got the whip..."

Just then, this big-'ol boy steps up from behind Larry. "Lil' Caesar," Larry's "big cousin," looked like he shoulda' already been startin' for St. Augustine High School or somethin'. Larry looked around at our faces, and knew some of us had our doubts.

"...it's not too late, no... Y'all could still call the game right now; we don't have to play a down if y'all don't want to..."

I got indignant,

"...WHAT? 'CUZ YOU GOT 'TOO-TALL JONES ON YOUR SIDE?! ...Y'all know that boy's B.F.N... BIG FUH NOTHIN! ...boy don't you

know? Haven't you heard? WE THE
BLOODHOUNDS FROM BACK-A-TOWN, AND
THE BLOODHOUNDS FROM BACK-A-TOWN
DON'T BACK DOWN!"

I don't remember in real-time. Everything
seems to come to my mind like as if it had
happened in slow motion—like a movie or
somethin'. What we did on that day, was
somethin' we'd all look upon later with pride...

The Bloodhounds came to play, and touch
football was the furthest thing from any of our
minds. Unlike when we were in Back-a-town
playin' in the middle of Duels Street, this was
Dillard's playing fields, where Dillard used to
practice and play when they had a team decades
before. We didn't dare play tackle football on the
streets—not because we couldn't handle fallin' in
the street, but because we would get our behinds
tore up by our mama's for tearin' holes in our
pants! So at Dillard, *tackle football* was the only
way to go. Besides... at Dillard, we could wear
our equipment...

We lost the toss, so we had to give them the
ball first. Mark had an arm like a rocket, so when
it was time to kick off; we chose to serve the ball
instead. And as always, we started our victory
chant before every kickoff— whether we won the
toss or not. It was what people at Auston's church

choir called, a "call-and-response." Big Ed, Jr. started it off.

"BLOODHOUNDS?!"

"YEAHHHHHH?!"

"WE GOT DA' WHIP!"

"YEAHHHH!!"

"I SAY BLOODHOUNDS?!"

"YEAHHHH?!"

"WE GOT THE COMP!"

"SAY BLOODHOUNDS?!"

"YEAHHHH?!"

"I GOT A QUESTION…"

"WHAT?!"

"WHO DAT SAY THEY GON' BEAT 'DEM

BLOODHOUNDS? WHO DAT?!... WHO

DAT?!"

"WHO DAT SAY THEY GON' BEAT 'DEM

BLOODHOUNDS? WHO DAT?!... WHO DAT?!"

"Who Dat" was the chant of every Black park football team in New Orleans' NORD (New Orleans Recreational Department) system—but it started in the 7th ward, and spread in both directions, to the 9th ward and to uptown. As it would turn out, Conrad, Shakespeare, and Harrell parks would get the reputation for it— that is, until years later, a certain NFL team would start doin' it—WITH THE WRONG RHYTHM!.

As we chanted and we beat our thigh pads to the rhythm of Ed's voice, we all got into position. Mark looked closely over the field to where Larry had everybody lined up. He never just threw any ball anywhere—it always had a purpose and a plan. Randy and Aubry were their fastest men. They had Gerald, Caesar, Larry on the front line, with Aubry on the left and Benny on the right on their middle line. Randy was by himself in the back. Since Mark knew he could throw it a lot further than anybody could kick it, he got a runnin' start, leaned back, and heaved that ball like it was just a rock or somethin'. Auston got tripped up by Gerald and it seemed like he would never stop rollin' down the field. Ed ran headlong into Caesar and, gettin' lower than him took him right up off his feet! If we weren't so intent on gettin' at Randy, we all might've stopped and had a big laugh right then. Nobody else from their team got a clear shot at the rest of us as we sped downfield. That ball hung up in the air so long there was no way Randy could field it and start runnin' it back. He kept lookin' for it to come down, like a dog waitin' for a tree' d cat. By the time he started hearin' our footsteps he got smart and decided to fair catch it. But when it hit his hands and bounced off, I was standin' right in his face, and recovered the ball.

'Dem boys was SICK! SICK about it! The Bloodhounds had the ball on about their fifteen yard line! Mark was our quarterback. As he barked out the signals, Big Ed, Jr. gots into his stance over the ball. I came in motion, and then as the ball was snapped, I ran hard at Larry, faked high, and hit 'em low, knocking his legs out from under him. I twisted my body as I hit him, so I could see him flyin' over the top of me. Meanwhile, Mark spotted Danny in the left corner of the end zone and he lobbed a back-shoulder pass over the top of Randy and Aubry. Danny let the ball fall into his outstretched arms lifted up the ball over his head. We went NUTS! Danny finished it off by pointing at Aubry and Randy, tauntin'em!

But they came to play too... After we served again, Randy didn't drop the ball. So six plays later, Larry got the snap from Aubry, and pitched out to Randy, deep in the backfield. Lil' Caesar pulled from the left to the right, as Randy followed him and Benny around the end. This time they all but run over Big Ed, Jr., Auston, Will, and me as Randy walked into the end zone, doing his "Billy white-shoes Johnson" dance .

"The Bloodhounds" and the "across the way boys" played that day like they were engaged in mortal combat. Each team scored against the other with purpose, with fury…with what Mr. Willie would call **adulation**.

Late in the game, the score was tied at 42 apiece… 48 was "game." So, the first team to score next would be the winner…

We were huddled up on defense-- the "across the way boys" on offense. It was 4th down, and Larry's team had to score either in order to win, or give up the ball on downs. From our huddle, we strained our ears to hear what they were plannin' to do. All we heard was,

"Awright, y'all know what to do. Randy, you…"

The rest of his plan was inaudible… so we got down to our plan. Just as Mark ran the offense, I was the one who came up with our defensive plans and schemes. I knew all of their tendencies, their habits… stupid things they did to give the play away, like Caesar changin' his stance to let you know which way they were gonna run or pass the ball...I decided we'd just rush Big Ed, Jr., and put everybody else back in coverage, 'cuz I thought we had em matched pretty good.

"Ed, you gotta get in there and get to Larry before he can get the ball off..."

"Can you get him?" added Auston.

"I got 'im y'all," said Big Ed, Jr. "He ain't gonna get away this time..."

"...you'd better, or we finished..." Auston continued.

Danny whispered to both of 'em;

"Shut up y'all!"

I told Mark to switch with me and let me take Randy while he covered Aubry. But Mark didn't seem so sure that I could cover Randy—even though he was their fastest man, I had him all day—sort of...

"Johnny, you sure you want me to switch with you?"

"Yeah, I got Randy... I'm gonna shut him down...

"Okay. So it's Man to man, with Big Ed, Jr. on the blitz, right?"

"Right," I said. "Ready?"

"BREAK!"

The atmosphere was so tense you could'a cut it with a knife. Randy lined up opposite me. He looked a little confused at first—like, "why isn't Mark out here?" But he looked at me and as he settled on his stance, he started to smile. What would follow played out like a scene from NFL Films or somethin'. The ball was snapped, and Randy took off, straight up the field. I got a good chuck on him off the line, so he couldn't really get loose like he might'a thought. I'd covered him before and I knew that he thought he could just flat outrun me. He was wrong… I was with him step for step—for the first twenty yards or so. Then, Randy cut to his right and for a second, I lost him—now he had two steps on me, but I wasn't givin' up. As we ran, Larry dropped back to throw the pass to what he thought was a wide open Randy. Big Ed was comin' down hard on Larry, as Caesar couldn't hold his block and Gerald fell down. Ed was closin' in on Larry, but…somehow, Big Ed Jr., missed Larry and he just heaved the ball into the air. Because he thought Ed would still hit him, Larry didn't get set, so the ball was flailin' — it was gonna fall short! It was right where I needed it to be! Randy would have to interfere with me to get the ball because it was COMIN' RIGHT TO ME! As I slowed down to make my jump for the ball... I don't know...it could'a been a hole in the turf or somethin'... all I now is...

I fell...

I could see the ball, at first comin' right to me, but now... floatin' over my outstretched hands and head as I fell out of position to get the ball. It grazed the top of my hand and it landed right in Randy's open hands...

Danny and Will were runnin' down field, after Randy ... others dove at his feet, but Randy juked left, then right as Auston fell to the ground. Randy outran Danny to the end zone for the winnin' score.

It all played out in slow motion, Randy runnin' into the end zone with Danny and Will chasin' behind him... Larry getting' up off the ground jumpin' and screamin'; Big Ed Jr., on the ground lookin' up in disbelief; Caesar and Benny and Gerald and Aubry all runnin' toward the end zone, jumpin' up and down and screamin' to the top of their lungs... Mark, taken out of the play by Aubry's route, and Auston, who was lookin' at me like he could kill me 2000 times over...

But *we woulda' beat them boys* if Big Ed, Jr. hit Larry before he got the ball off...or if Danny or Will or Auston woulda' caught Randy-- he really wasn't that fast...

...final Score..."Cross the way," 48..."Back-a-town," 42...

That's how it was in those days, a real nail-biter...full of suspense and drama...

The walk back to Danny and Will's place seemed to take forever. Nobody said a thing the whole way back. Once we got back, we all started sittin' our equipment down and sat on their front porch. The silence was deafnin'… then, Mark broke the silence.

"...what you gonna do tomorrow?"

"...I dunno... Maybe go swimmin after church..."

"...ya' need to cool off after gettin' burned the way Randy burnt you today!" Auston was ready to start mess---again…

"Shut up, man!" yelled Danny.

"It's true, we never woulda' lost if he didn't "mysteriously" fall down!"

Big Ed, Jr. came to my defense,

"That ain't fair, Auston..."

"Fair?! Your big butt couldn't get to Larry, like you said you would, that's how he got the pass down field in the first place!"

"I...I got a piece of 'im..."

"Well a "piece" wasn't good enough, was it?"

Mark had heard enough...

"Okay, Auston, I mean it, SHUT UP!"

"SHUT DON'T GO UP, PRICES DO, so take my advice and SHUT UP TOO!"

Auston barely got the last word out before Mark had jumped on him, pushing Auston to the ground. Auston tried to get up to fight, but the rest of the BLOODHOUNDS knew Mark would kill'em—so we jumped in to hold him as well as Mark.

"AWRIGHT! STOP IT MAN, STOP IT!" I said. Big Ed was right at my side.

"YEAH! We boys, man. Cool out, Auston! We a team..."

"I HATE losin' to them! I HATE IT! ...All this talk about bein' Bloodhounds and not backin' down! It's a buncha'...

LOOK AT US... for all our talk; we ain't beat d'em boys in 6 months! We sad, man...SAD! ...we don't even have full uniforms... You call this a TEAM?!

Auston threw what was left of his equipment to the ground, and ran home. Big Ed, Jr. was really startin' to get mad now... he got up and yelled after Auston.

"GO ON, RUN HOME! YOU DOIN' JUS' LIKE LARRY SAID, RUNNIN' HOME LIKE SOME POO-PUTT! GO ON!

"Big Ed, Jr. cool it, man... Let 'im go..."

"But he KNOWS we need him to be able to play them boys in the rematch..."

"Yeah, he knows and he don't care... I say, let 'im go... He don't need to be a bloodhound if he don't want..."

"No y'all, we can't be that way... Aus, been with us from the jump..."

"I don't know 'bout y'all, but I'm not gonna be runnin' behind none-a-y'all! Not Auston, not none-a-y'all! C'mon, Ed…"

Mark stormed off, leaving his helmet and pads behind. Big Ed, Jr. followed slowly behind, looking behind him at me, and Danny and Will. Danny, who'd been simmerin' all this time, finally let it out.

"…Why's everybody always cryin' 'bout everything? I'm goin' inside Will…you comin'?!"

Will looked at Danny, and then at me, try'na make sense of the last few minutes. He looked to me for some sign… some reassurance… that THE BLOODHOUNDS are not disbandin'. I tried to smooth things over…my voice cracked a little.

"…they jus' mad for now… They'll be awright, just wait, you'll see…"

Danny was still mad — he could always make Will do stuff when he really didn't't' want to.

"Will?! C'mon, it's late anyhow…"

Will didn't wanna go, I could tell… But he nodded at me, picked up his ball and the rest of their equipment, and headed inside. The squeaky screen door closed behind him, and for the first time in a long time, I stood out in front of that house by myself. The streetlights just started to come on and like it always was in Back-a-town, you were 'sposed to be inside by nightfall. So I picked up Aus and Mark's equipment that they left on the walkway and started for home. I got to my front porch and started to open the door… but I couldn't… I felt like as if goin' inside for the night meant I was givin' up on the day, and I just couldn't let that happen, not a day like the one we just had—I just couldn't give up on The Bloodhounds.

So, I headed for Mr. Willie and Miss Verna's. They had always been there for us in the past and I just knew they would be now. No matter what we had to face they always had an answer for our problems and this was a BIG problem…

CHAPTER 3

I knew I hadn't asked permission from my mama or my daddy to go down to Mr. Willie's. I knew I could get in a lotta trouble. But I didn't care. I just needed somebody who knew us...who *knew* The Bloodhounds... to be able to tell me what I needed to do to fix things. So I went to the side of the store, on the North Dorgenois Street side, 'cuz it was the side of the store towards the back, where the door was to where Mr. Willie and Miss Verna actually lived upstairs. I was so desperate, I was knockin' on the door and ringin' the bell like our lives depended on it. And in a sense, that's exactly how it was.

It seemed like it was takin' forever for somebody to come to the door. Then, I could hear the window upstairs bein' messed with, like somebody was fightin' with the window latch. A light came on in that window, and it finally came up with Miss Verna's head stickin' out.

"Johnny? ...it's late baby, what's the matter?"

"I... Can I come up and talk to Mr. Willie...and to you?"

She seemed to pause for a minute, like she was
try'na read the look on my face. One thing was
for sure, she knew somethin' had to be the matter
if I was at her door that time a evenin' when I
knew I was gonna get my butt whipped for bein'
out too late.

"Sure baby, come on. I'll let ya people know
ya' here."

Miss Verna, in her lime-green housecoat with
matching Daniel Green slippers, opened the door
and let me in.

All the years I had been comin' over by Mr.
Willie and Miss Verna's store, I had never been
upstairs in their house. I don't think anybody I
knew had ever been up there. It was like taking a
walk back through time or somethin' — there were
sooo many pictures everywhere! Even though it
looked like a typical 7th ward shotgun house on
the outside, on the inside it was much more. I
always used to like history, (and math), and this
house was full of history. In their living room,
there were pictures of Mr. Willie and Miss Verna
when they were little — family portraits and
individual pictures…you could tell they got 'em
done at a portrait studio somewhere, like A.P.
Bedou. There were pictures of Mr. Willie as a
young man, both in school and in his service
uniform. Some of Miss Verna's pictures on the

wall ranged from first communion portraits by Mr. Bedou, to Mardi Gras pictures with the "Dancing Dolls," and with Big Chief "Tootie" Montana. There were also pictures of when they were "courtin' each other, their wedding pictures, and the pictures of their kids and grandkids. What walls weren't covered with pictures had bookcases that ran almost floor-to-ceiling with books, encyclopedias, manuals, and novels.

I must've spun around like a spinnin' top, but in slow motion, lookin' at all of the history, all of the warmth, and all of the love in that room.

"Ya' want something to eat, baby...some dinner, or maybe some cookies?"

"No ma'am...thanks though..."

"Johnny?"

Mr. Willie was sittin' leaned back in his old lazyboy — that chair looked older than both of 'em and it was so different, like it didn't belong in a house with so much history. He was sittin' there in just an undershirt, and his khaki, Dickie's, work pants.

"... What brings my lead "Bloodhound" up here?"

"...there ain't no more "Bloodhounds," Mr. Willie."

"No more "Bloodhounds?!" Boy, you talkin'
crazy!

"No, Mr. Willie... There ain't no more
"Bloodhounds." We split up...gone our separate
ways..."

"Split up? You better not talk like that, no...
Y'all ain't splittin' nothin'... Y'all need to be
splittin' heads on 'dem cross the way boys..."

"Willie, don't talk 'round that boy like that..."
said Miss Verna. "He'll end up doin' it..."

"Son, you know I don't mean, 'literally'?"

"Yeah... I guess so..."

"See Verna Mae, nothin' to worry about..."

Mr. Willie took a long pause... like he was
studyin' me. It's funny; Miss Verna seemed to do
the same thing when I was knockin' at the door
earlier. Ol' folks had a way a' readin'
people...sizing them up, or maybe try'na figure
out where they were really comin' from. I kinda
started gettin' uncomfortable when he finally
spoke.

"So, what seems to be the problem?"

I started off slow, talkin' about the game and the fight afterwards and everything, all of it... and the longer I talked, the faster I talked, and the madder I got.

"Well... We lost to Larry and his boys today... Big Ed, Jr. couldn't get to Larry before Larry got the ball off, and Auston and Danny's supposed to be so fast, but they couldn't catch Randy, and Will dropped 2 passes right in his hands!"

Mr. Willie looked at me like he was waitin' to hear somethin' else...like I hadn't told the "whole truth" about what happened at Dillard that day. So he just sat there... waitin' on me, and I just sat there...waitin' on him, and *we just sat there*...

"AWRIGHT...I...I fell down on the last play of the game and Randy caught the ball and ended up scoring...and later we got into arguments and Mark pushed Auston and everybody jus' got mad and walked off..."

It felt like a big weight off my chest...*finally*...

"...and I don't know what to do, Mr. Willie, I don't know how to keep the Bloodhounds together..."

Mr. Willie just sat there, takin' it all in. It seemed to be an eternity... Was he gonna blame me for it?

Was all a' this my fault? Could I fix it? — he leaned forward in his recliner,

"First of all...it ain't *YOUR JOB* to keep the Bloodhounds together...they wanna go, let 'em go..."

"...That's what Mark said..."

"Your real friends will always come back...they just gotta blow off some steam, and think about where they were wrong, even if they don't admit it to you..."

"...Yeah, like Auston...he can't stand bein' wrong..."

"Yeah, there's always at least one in ev'ry bunch,"

"Baby, you know what?" Miss Verna joined the conversation. "Willie and I had friends we came up with, even friends who were married like us... We all used to hang together, play pokeno, tonk and pitty-pat on Friday nights, and things... We thought of formin' our own club, you know, like the Autocrat or the Titan Club...We had some good times, yeah... But what we didn't know was one of the husbands in the group, Randall Romain; he was messin' around on his wife, Judy... Judy thought Willie, and one of the other men, Bernard Rush, knew about it, 'cuz they all worked at the post office at the time..."

"But what she didn't know was, Randall Romain was a real smooth one..." Added Mr. Willie. "He was lyin' to us about her and lyin to her about ev'rything... whooo!"

"Well son, once she found out he was cheatin' on her, she had a fit, and she blamed Willie, Bernard, the other wives, she had enough blame to spread around ev'rybody...there was so much mess in the group, we decided it was better to break it up... Only Willie and I, Bernard and his wife, Mark and Michael's dad and mama, were the only ones who remained friends... So what am I sayin' baby?"

They kinda lost me at the "messin' around" part. So, Miss Verna continued.

"Ev'ry relationship, mama, daddy, brothers and sisters, especially friends— is tested...tried and tested with mess, to show you where your heart is with them, and where their hearts are with you...it never fails...every REAL relationship goes through some trials..."

"...ev'ry trial tells you where you stand... Most times folks make their mistakes by puttin' people in the wrong place in relation to themselves... See that chessboard?"

Mr. Willie pointed to an old black and white marbled chess set he had on the coffee table behind me. We got up and walked over to the table.

"...ya see this knight? I got choices about where to move him, or if I wanna move him at all right now, see? Now, if I move him here..."

Mr. Willie moved the piece into a part of the board where he knew it could be captured.

"...then you can take him by movin' the bishop from here..."

And just as he said, he captured the black knight with my white bishop.

"I put my piece in the wrong place, and it got taken, see? ...relationships are just like that...we take people who should be "acquaintances" or just people we know, and make 'em best friends, because that's what *WE* want, then we get mad at them and ev'rybody else when they hurt us... They were NEVER qualified to be our best friends..."

It was as if I had heard it for the first time. I never thought about anybody qualifyin' for bein' my friend, like it was for a job or somethin'. To me, people either were my friends or they weren't. So the idea of these guys I knew all of my life: Mark, Danny, Will, Auston, and Ed...the thought of me havin' to "qualify them"…I didn't know what to do with that.

"Now," said Mr. Willie, "concerning the Bloodhounds... I really think y'all will get back together…and soon..."

It felt as if the entire Superdome had been lifted off my chest! I almost jumped up from the chair, when Mr. Willie added,

"...but wait now, hold ya' horses son...don't get too excited too soon..."

I sat back down, and Mr. Willie continued.

"...give 'em time, like I said... You guys've taken this loss to them other kids real hard, REAL HARD... It might take a while for some, longer for others...in the end you'll know who passed the test, okay..."

"Okay, Mr. Willie, I understand... we all just need some time..."

"That's right baby," Miss Verna added, "…a lil' time apart won't hurt nothin'...'sides, don'tchu have that lil' Desvigne girl you could be spendin' time with?"

SHE know'about MARIE?!

"How did you..."

"What... Ya' think we "too old? — We could teach you a thing or two about courtin'..."

Mr. Willie came to my rescue,

"...Now Verna Mae, you know that boy is too young for..."

"Oh stop it Willie, you was younger than him when you was chasin' me around...and makin' eyes, and stuff..."

I was glad the subject shifted just enough offa' me and Marie.

"Did your mama run Mr. Willie away like Marie's Nanain does?

Miss Verna fell out laughin'

"Oh, no!... My mama LOVED her some WILLIE! In her eyes, he couldn't do no wrong... Hunh, if she only knew..."

Mr. Willie could sense that his wife was about to take this conversation in a direction that he did *not* want it to go.

"Oh, but that's another story for another day, son... It's late, and I KNOW your mama's gonna be concerned, even though we already told her you was here..."

Miss Verna asked if I needed a ride 'cuz it was late. But I really didn't have that far to go.

"No, Miss Verna's right," Mr. Willie insisted, "you comin' with me..."

A few minutes later, Mr. Willie's car pulled up to the curb in front of my house. My mama was there, standin' in the front door, waving to Mr. Willie. Before I got out, Mr. Willie leaned over and said,

"Awright, we're here...remember what I said...your real friends will always come back..."

I nodded my head, got out of the car, and started walking toward my house.

"I just hope we do all get back together...I'm just afraid...

Mr. Willie wouldn't let me finish that thought.

"What?! You a BLOODHOUND aren't ya'?! He knew who we were and what we stood for.

"BLOODHOUNDS..."

"Don't back down!

"That's my boy! He Said, "Go on now..."

Even though we lost the game, now I couldn't
wait to get back to school on Monday. I had high
hopes for the Bloodhounds...and I couldn't wait
to see Marie Desvigne again...

On Monday, Mark and me didn't talk that much
at all that day, even though we were both in Mrs.
Goldwater's class. Mrs. Goldwater was a 7th
grade teacher from hell. She ran her classroom
like a boot-camp, with flawless lines, and desks
lined up with perfection. She tolerated no noise
during her classes. During our last exam, I was
almost done, so I was bored outta my mind. I
started to sneak looks at Mark, who was probably
ignoring me. When she observed her class, Mrs.
Goldwater acted like a hawk lookin' for its next
meal...she didn't tolerate any foolishness. And
there I was, lookin' around the room when she
already said for us not to... After all, we *were*
testing.

"Johnny Walters...if I see your eyes roving
around my classroom again, you will have to
explain to Sister AND your parents why you got
a "zero" on my exam. Is that clear to you, son?"

I slowly nodded to MRS. GOLDWATER, and returned to number 76 out of 105 questions on my exam…

…did I say I was BORED OUTTA MY MIND?!

After number 84, I started to sneak looks at Marie Desvigne. I really liked her, and *I knew she liked me too.*

Mrs. Goldwater was in the middle of grading those exams when a note came to her from the office. She always got this really annoyed look on her face whenever somethin' broke her concentration…like the world was gonna end or somethin'. She picked up the note,

"Johnny Walters and Mark Doucre…report to the main office…NOW!

Under her breath, I could hear her mumble',

"…saved by the Father…again…"

Mark and I got up and headed out to the office. On the way there, I wanted to say somethin' but I couldn't. He didn't say a word either. When we got to the office, we found out what the reason was — we weren't in trouble. We got called out from class again to do another funeral with Fr. Mike. Fr. Michael McCabe was a cool priest — and he always got us checked out during math class. Besides it bein' math and bein' kinda easy to me, the only other thing I liked about math class was that Mark and Marie were in there, and it was scheduled at the same time that the priests had to serve funerals. That meant we ALWAYS got out from her class!

Servin' Funerals were always a mixed bag to me. On the one hand, people were always so sad — at least, that was at Catholic funerals. The Baptist funerals I'd been to with Auston were always a lotta people jumpin' and shoutin' — some cryin' too. But always more, I dunno, joyful…on the other hand, we got to miss some of Mrs. Goldwater's math class, we got to ride in a big, black or silver limousine, and Father Mike always paid us some money after we served.

After school I was on my way home and the quickest way for me to get there is past Danny and Will's house. As I walked slowly in front of their house, and could see Mark walking on the other side of the street, to his house. He never stopped; he never said a word, not even eye contact. Normally, we'd meet up at Danny and Will's house after school, hang out, maybe play some football or cool-can in the street…I know Mr. Willie said it would take some time, but right now…nobody seemed interested… It looked like the BLOODHOUNDS finally backed down… *and broke down…*

We just finished the last day of school, the last official day of 7th grade. We'd have almost three months before we'd have to be back at school again. But when we returned, we'd be full-fledged 8th graders...Yet, I wasn't excited about it... I missed the Bloodhounds...

And I was *really* gonna miss Marie...

She didn't live in Back-a-town, and I'd only get to see her if she went by her Nanain and Parrain's house, around the corner... "Nanain" and "Parrain" are your "God-mother" and "God-father..." I used to try and sneak over there, but Marie's Nanain was real mean...and the back of her house was next to the back of Wendy Marchand's house...

...and *who* was Wendy Marchand?

Wendy used to like me, but I didn't "like" her — *not like that*. She always talked bad about Marie behind her back, for no reason...

...jealous I guess...

...besides that, her hair was always lookin' "pas-yais"...

...that means her head was lookin' "whipped!"

It didn't matter if you had straight hair, curly hair, or nappy hair; you better not leave your house with it lookin' "pas-yais"...

"...no comb? –Then don't leave home..."

And yet Wendy Marchand had the nerve to always be talkin' 'bout *somebody else's hair*... Like as if she had hers lookin' good or somethin'...

My mama used to say, "...if she felt better about herself, she probably wouldn't be so insecure..., and people might like her more." The only reason I'd go anywhere around Wendy Marchand's house is 'cuz I could sneak into Wendy's backyard to see if I could get to see Marie one more time. So I snuck in through the Marchand's chain link gate, and went to their back wall where there were some scattered cinder blocks. I stacked some of the blocks one on top the other and I got up on them, pulling myself up so I could see over the edge of the wall.

Marie's bedroom window faced the Marchand's back wall – it was only about 10 or 12 feet away. I jumped down off the blocks and picked up a handful of loose pebbles from the yard, and stuffed them in my right pants pocket. Once I got myself back up on the wall, I started throwin' the pebbles against MARIE'S window. The first three times, nothin' happened. But the fourth time, I saw the curtains movin'! I ducked

down a little…in case it was Ol' Miss Desvigne.
But it wasn't…

…it was Marie!

She came to the rear window, started waving and
smiling with that big, pretty smile. And I smiled
and waved back. She opened the window,

"I'd hoped you would come by to see me
before I left, Johnny…"

I couldn't speak… Hearing Marie actually TALK
TO ME for the first time outside of school left me
speechless! Her voice was so soft, so cultured. It's
funny, our parents stressed speaking properly,
and we did it in school and in public, but we
talked *like we talked* when we were with friends.
Marie talked to me, like as if we'd been talkin'
forever…

"…Ya' know, my mama and daddy are
supposed to be picking me up this evening…
I'll be staying back uptown for the summer…"

I was still speechless, still frozen… Marie
continued, as if we were really having a
conversation or somethin'.

"…So, that means I probably won't see you all
summer long…that is…unless, they let me
spend some time over here during the

summer... what do you think Johnny... Would you like that?"

*"Would I like that..."*ARE YOU KIDDIN' ME?! That was what I was sayin' in my mind, 'cuz nothin' was comin' outta my mouth! This was EVERYTHING I'D HOPED FOR! Yes, YES! I WOULD OVE THAT!

I tried to say somethin' I could see her lookin' for an answer from me, but...

...crickets...

Then...

"MAMAAAAAAAAAA!!!"

My reverie was shattered by the screams of a jealous, crazy girl with "pas-yais" hair! Wendy Marchand was screamin' at the top of her lungs and when I spun around, I remembered what I was standin' on...

The bricks and I, like the walls of Jericho from the Bible, came tumblin' down. All at once I was scared, mad, and hurt... because I didn't get a chance to finally tell Marie Desvigne how I felt...

...and because my knee and my shoulder REALLY HURT! I wheeled around, holdin' my knee with one hand and my shoulder with the other.

"WENDY MARCHAND! WHATCHU DID THAT FOR?!"

Wendy wailed,

"YOU WANNA TALK TO MARIE, YOU NEED TO GO TO HER HOUSE! NOT SNEAKIN' AROUND MY BACKYARD...

MAMAAAAAAAAAA!"

Wendy's mother, Mrs. Marchand, came into the yard, as Marie's Nanain pulled Marie out of the rear window. I was terrified. She pulled me up by the same arm I fell on and she started whippin' me *in her back yard*!

I knew I must've really liked Marie... 'cuz I totally forgot that my mama didn't want me ANYWHERE near Wendy Marchand's back yard, because she didn't really like Mrs. Marchand. But that didn't mean Mrs. Marchand couldn't beat my behind...and Because Mrs. Marchand beat my behind... My mama was gonna do double...

My mama's smile, when she "received me" from some other adult for doin' somethin' I shouldn't have, was strictly a formality—a way to let them know she appreciated someone lookin' out for her boy... and a way to let me know *my behind belonged to her*!

Back then, every black woman in the 7th ward whipped their children the same way. It was this vocal and rhythmic, syncopated thing they did where every time they went on a down stroke with the belt, or the hairbrush, or especially the Daniel Green slipper — whatever they found close...

"WHAT, DID I, TELL, YOU, ABOUT, GOIN', IN MISS MARCHAND'S, YARD!

Then she'd catch a breath...

"DON'T, EVER, LET, ME, CATCH, YOU, DOIN', WHAT, I, TOLD, YOU NOT TO, DO, DON'T DO IT, DON'T DO IT, DON'T...DO IT!"

But punishment was far from over, 'cuz Mr. Walters, already informed by phone of my latest exploits, was takin' his belt off for me as he hit the front door.

"JOHNNYYYYY!!"

...and whatever my mama did, my daddy did triple that... That's how it was in those days — everybody had an "interest" in your well-being...

.

...I could'a stood a whole lot less "interest" if you know what I mean..."

Even with whippin's like I got that day and night...I couldn't wait to see Marie again...

After three days on punishment — no outside, no TV, no playin' in the house, just chores, and sittin' in my room, I was sittin' in the rear window of this bedroom, lookin' through my yard, and seein' Auston playing in his backyard, trying not to look in my direction.

"Johnny?" My mama called from the kitchen.

"Yes mama."

"What are you doin'?"

"Just sittin' here… I cleaned up my room like you said."

She follows my voice into my room, watchin' me at the window.

"I see that... baby, you did a good job..."

I didn't say anything back, but I could tell she was still standin' in my doorway. Silence from mama in these situations always meant she was thinkin' about somethin' else — somethin' more on her mind besides my room, or what I was doin'

"I know that you, know your father and I
mean what's best for you...and I know you realize
we had to discipline you, because you know
what's at stake, and you know that people need to
know you LISTEN when we say something..."

I nodded, "yes ma'am."

"...what I'm trying to say is...you represent
this family when you're out there, and ev'rybody
knows and expects that of you...you can't just do
*what you wanna do when you wanna do it and
not have consequences*...it's all a part of life..."
She changes the subject in mid-stream, as if the
last few minutes never happened.

"...I need you to go to Mr. Willie and Miss
Verna's and get me a carton of eggs, a half-gallon
of milk, and a half-a-pound of hog-head cheese..."

She gave me the money then quickly changes
back to her previous conversation.

"...remember...*you* represent **US**...you
represent black people...wherever you go, people
may not know your name, but they know you're a
black boy... And if they know your name, they
know you're a Walters...That means somethin'
son...

Before she would bring me the money and the grocery list, she started to close my bedroom door, and leave me to my own thoughts…

"…that *means somethin'*…"

So, just like that I was off punishment, and back on the streets of Back-a-town — but with a lot more wisdom…

…and a lot sorer behind…

It's funny how old folks used to say, "Love will make a man do some crazy things…" I finally decided I would get comfortable with the fact that I was in love with Marie Desvigne, and no amount of public humiliation at the hands of Mrs. Marchand was gonna change that. So while people pointed at me and laughed about the public whippin' I got from Mrs. Marchand, it didn't even matter…'cuz I was *in love*…

I was still thinkin' about Marie's last words to me: "…would you like that?" I felt warm all over, still rememberin' her smile…

I was within one block of the store, at the corner of Hope and Allen Streets, when my joy daydream was shattered…

Pop!

Pop!

For a minute I just froze — try'na add up in
my mind whether it was a car engine backfirin'
or... no... it wasn't... I started runnin'. In spite
of everything my parents ever taught me,
everything they told me about gunshots and
trouble... that I was always *supposed* to run *away*
from the shots, I began to run toward the sound
of the shots. I ran as fast as I could... as if I almost
knew what I would find when I got there. By the
time I got to Law and Allen Street, at the corner of
the park, I could see the thick, black smoke
billowing from the broken picture window and
from the spaces alongside the window air
conditioning unit, and from the front entrance of
Mr. Willie and Miss Verna's store. Two thugs ran
from the store and vanished around the corner.
Mr. Willie stumbled out behind them, pistol in
hand, holding around his stomach area. Before he
could get a shot off, he collapsed to the ground. I
just froze again... it was as if time stood still...
It was the screams and then the crowd from
Hardin's baseball field spillin' out from the park
onto the street that brought me out of it.

"MR. WILLIE! MR. WILLIEEEEEE!"

People kept runnin' from the baseball park and
from the pool, and I rushed to where Mr. Willie
had fallen.

The police and firemen moved through the
crime scene like ants on a picnic, while other
officers kept bystanders well away from the site.
The store suffered severe fire and smoke damage,
as well as Mr. Willie and Miss Verna's home
above it. Miss Verna wasn't there when it
happened. Her sister brought her to Charity
Hospital, where they took Mr. Willie. Police
started to scatter throughout the crowd, lookin'
for potential witnesses, searchin' for any clues to
the identities of the gunmen.

"Did you see what they were wearing?"

"I...I didn't see nuthin' officer," said one of the
bystanders, "I just saw when Willie stumbled out
of the door and fell on the sidewalk..."

"Are you sure? There isn't anything you can
remember?"

"All's I know is, I saw the smoke, and heard
the shots... no... maybe I heard the shots first then
saw the smoke... I...I Don't know Officer...is Willie
gonna be awright?"

I had to walk away... I couldn't hear
anymore... I saw my mama and my daddy
runnin' toward me. All I could do was run to
them, and cry...I never felt so full...and so empty
at the same time...What if Mr. Willie didn't pull
through? What would Miss Verna do now?

I felt like I cried for hours. I must've fallen asleep because it was night time. I could hear my parents in the kitchen, talking about Mr. Willie, Miss Verna, and the community.

"Mona...'You know that Willie and Verna are under-insured?"

"What? You' gotta be kiddin' Stan..."

"No, it's no joke...They say they're "severely" under-insured. Mr. Thomas, Meeks' insurance agent, said that they have substantial damage to the store, and that the combination of the store repairs and the lost income from the store will be higher than the coverage. Willie might not pull through, and even if he does, the store won't be cleared by code enforcement in time for Willie and Verna to be able to pay their mortgage."

I got up from my bed and pushed my door open a little further to hear their conversation. My mama asked,

"...you mean, even if Willie pulls through, they can still lose their store?"

"Yeah, baby... They might lose it all..."

My father's last words swirled around inside my head like a bad song that just wouldn't go away. "...they might lose it all..." It was a nightmare on top of the nightmares of the entire day. I could lose a man who was like a grandfather to me, to the whole community — a man who had a big heart and who loved people. He was all that and so much more.

He was my friend…

…And no one let's a friend, or his dream just die.

So I closed my door, put on my shoes, and climbed out of my bedroom window, into the back yard, headin' to Mark's house. We hadn't spoken since the game at Dillard. I hesitated for a minute about knocking on Mark's bedroom window...but when I thought about Mr. Willie and Miss Verna… *"Love will make a man do crazy things…"*

"Mark… Mark?" I tapped lightly on the window with a pebble from the yard. Michael, Mark's younger, freckled-faced brother, came to the window instead. He kinda' caused me to jump back from the window.

"Johnny?! What'chu doin'? Yo' mama's gonna kill you!"

"Is Mark Up?" I whispered.

"Hold on…"

At first, I thought he might've forgotten me, he took so long…or maybe he was havin' trouble wakin' Mark up — he slept like a brick. But a few minutes later, Mark came to the window, lookin' sleepy and irritated.

"Johnny? What'chu want? It's late man…"

"Did you hear about Mr. Willie?

"Yeah, my mama and daddy were talkin' about it this evening… Me and Mike been by our cousins in Vascoville all day today…"

"Did you hear Mr. Willie might not live and even if he does, they don't have enough money to keep the store?"

When I told him that, it woke Mark right up outta his sleep.

"Whaddaya mean, might not make it?"

"Mark, he got shot in the stomach…they say it's a nasty wound and even though they stopped the bleeding, he could still die."

"…and what about the store?

"I heard my mama and daddy say, that even if Mr. Willie pulls through the hospital, they don't have enough insurance to fix up the store from the fire. ...if they can't fix up the store enough, the city won't let 'em open back up...and if they can't open back up, they can't pay their note...and if they can't pay their note...they'll lose their place...we gotta do somethin' to help them..."

"...It's gonna take a lot-a-money."

"'What...you backin' down, Johnny?"

"No!"

"...So, The Bloodhounds are *back*?

Funny, he was askin' me, like I already knew or somethin'. I really didn't know what to think. We all never went this long without talkin'. Almost a week had gone by since the game.

"We gotta get the rest of the bloodhounds, but don't know if they'll..."

"They'll come...this is about Mr. Willie and Miss Verna..."

So we started roundin' ev'rybody up... Big Ed, Jr.... Danny and Will...

...and Auston was our last stop. He was the one most upset about everything, and he was always the hardest one to convince of anything that made sense—Auston was somebody who you couldn't talk into—or out of somethin' once he put his mind to it.

So we all snuck up to Auston's back window. Mark knocked on the window, while we stood look-out.

"Say you Auston? Wake up man... Wake up..."

Auston came slowly to his window, try'na shake off the sleep.

"Mark?...Johnny?.. Wha... What y'all doin' in my backyard?"

"'you heard about Mr. Willie?

"Yeah... 'folks say he's shot bad..."

"...and He might not make it...

"Mmm Hummm..."

"Aus...you heard they might lose their store too?

Auston really woke up at hearin' this.

"No... I mean...what will Miss Verna do?"

Big Ed, Jr. added,

"...she'd have to find somewhere else to live..."

"No more store?" said Auston.

"No more store..." said Danny. "...and that's whether Mr. Willie pulls through or not..." Now you could tell Auston was startin' to get scared.

"...you think he's gonna die?"

"They say he got shot in the stomach," Will added. "...people can die from that, Auston..."

Auston looked around at all the rest of the Bloodhounds all standin' outside his bedroom window. We all had our game faces on, and it was time he put his on too... he knew he was wrong for startin' the mess between us, and that we had to put all that behind us to help Mr. Willie and Miss Verna. It was time...

"...okay," said Auston. "So what do we do now, Bloodhounds?"

All of us said it at the same time, like we knew each other's thoughts...

"We <u>don't</u> back down..."

It was simple: Mr. Willie and Miss Verna needed money, and we needed to make some money… well…lots 'a money…So we started doin' everything we could to raise money for Mr. Willie and Miss Verna…

We went to Miss Mae, who went to her giant cookie jar, turned it over, and pulled off an envelope taped to the bottom. She took out $20 in small bills and handed it to me…

We sold stuff, like Auston's mama's old toaster…Danny sold some of his mama's famous peanut butter fudge to people like Coach Rollins.

The Bloodhounds set up a table at the edge of the parking lot at St. Matthews, and we sold lots of homemade cookies, candies, and potato chips in small sandwich bags. The parishioners were happy to oblige us…and last, but not least, the congregation of the Greater Mt. Zion Baptist Church, Where Mr. Willie and Miss Verna were members, let us put a donation box in the church especially for them. After service, church members passed by us, some giving money, while others give us an "at-a-boy" tap on our shoulders. Miss Verna came out of church with two of her friends — you could tell, she was happy about what we did.

…we would do anything for Mr. Willie and Miss Verna…

Later, we met back in Danny and Will's backyard. We started to empty out all that we'd collected on the wooden bench in the back of the yard. I emptied the bags and cans while Mark counted the money…we were all so anxious.

"How much we got, Mark?" The suspense was killin' me.

"A-hundred and ten dollars, aaannd…fifty-three cents.

"'That enough?" Big Ed was not the best at math.

"…are you kiddin' me man?!"Danny said.

"That ain't even close…"

Auston was startin' to get irate again… "Does anybody know how much we REALLY NEED?"

"A lot more that this Aus…" said Mark.

I was more precise. "…Thousands…"

"WHAT?!"

"We been at this for what, TWO WEEKS," said Auston, "We can't get THOUSANDS of dollars in a couple-a-weeks! Ain't that when the note on the store is due?"

Mark added, "...yeah, we don't have much more time."

"Well come on!" Auston pushed. "There's no way we can get that kind'a money... We just kids!"

I wasn't givin' up that easy...we were not *JUST KIDS*.

"NO! We're BLOODHOUNDS!"

"O yeah, and that means WHAT, Johnny?"

Like usual, Auston stormed off. Big Ed, Jr. paused a while, bowed his head in defeat, and followed him. Time seemed to stand still at Auston's question. As his words sank in deeper and deeper, The Bloodhounds begin to split up again.

"C'mon Will..." said Danny, "it's gettin' dark real fast..."

"But Danny?"

Danny gave Will that "get your butt up, NOW" look. Reluctantly, Will headed inside, leaving Mark and me alone.

"Johnny..." Mark began, "I...I think this time... Auston may be right..."

"RIGHT?! You gotta be kiddin' me man! Don't Mr. Willie and Miss Verna mean ANYTHING to you?! TO ANY OF YOU?!"

I was talkin' like everybody was still out there.

"These are people who been there for us... For everybody! We can't just turn our backs on 'em now..."

As if he didn't hear a word I had said, Mark began to walk off toward home. I was getting' madder an' madder every step he took...

"THEY NEED US!"

But, he wasn't' listenin'...So I yelled it even louder...

"THEY NEED US!"

I kicked the can and box we used to collect the money and I ran through Danny and Will's yard to the back fence, try'na use a shortcut through an open lot, toward home. I ran as fast as I could...as if runnin' could make me feel better, or make me forget that we were just kids and what could we do that the grown folks couldn't do to get that money? I was runnin' through the back lot, pass a row of parked cars when I tripped and fell on the ground. The sight I saw in front'a me made me forget about money, Mr. Willie, Miss Verna, EVERYTHING.

IT WAS COO-CORN BREAD!

As he started to reach for me, all I could say was...

"DON'T EAT ME! DON'T..."

"Don't... Don't be 'fraid a me..." he said.

I had never, NEVER in my life, heard Coo-Corn Bread speak before... His voice was...

Gentle...

I still wasn't sure though...

"You... you not gonna hurt me?"

"No... No I ain't, son... I heard what y'all been doin'... for Willie and Verna and all..."

I was shocked — I couldn't do nothin' else but sit there and listen.

"I... wanna try to help... help you..."

Now that I knew he wasn't gonna eat me, I started to get a little more courage.

"How! How you gonna help us...help them?"

"I know how you might get the money y'all need..."

He bent down toward me and started speaking in a whisper — as if somebody else would overhear.

"Go to Madame Muvalla's... on Royal Street, in the Quarter..."

"Madame who?"

"Muvalla... Mu-va-la... She got a voodoo shop in..."

VOODOO?! Did he know who I was?! Who my parents were?!What they would do to me if I went *ANYWHERE NEAR A VOODOO SHOP*?!
"Voodoo?!"

"Shhhhh! She just runs a voodoo shop... She don't practice it... 'folks say, she know 'bout a map...a map that leads to a lot a money..."

I wasn't sure 'bout any of this... Voodoo? Money? So, I asked him,

"Why...why she ain't got the money yet if she got the map?"

"I don't know... all's I know is they say she the one who got it..."

I got up from the ground now. Brushed myself off, and started to head toward home. Behind me, Coo-Corn Bread was still try'na convince me.

"She got that map, yeah. All's you gotta do is get it from her, and find that money..."

"find that money..."

I stopped and turned around to watch him walk off, still looking as if he was bein' watched or followed, until he disappeared again, into the shadows, behind an old house.

CHAPTER 4

I remember runnin'... from what, I don't know, all I know is, I had to keep runnin'. Fast as I could, I ran...through the streets, around parked cars, through alleyways. I fall into some trash cans lined up in the alley, but I can't hear myself fall down—I don't hear the sound of the cans, the garbage, the lids or myself, slammin' on the concrete. But it doesn't matter, 'cuz I can't let myself get caught. I gotta get up, and I gotta keep runnin'. I'm lookin' over my shoulder, but I still can't see who, *or what* is chasin' me, but *I can feel* it...

All of a sudden, I can see a man, a figure, almost like a shadow, comin' after me but now... I'm movin' in slow motion! No matter how hard I try, I can't seem to run like I need to run...and this thing is gainin' on me! I keep lookin' over my shoulder, and it's getting' closer, and bigger, and I'm try'na scream for help—but no sound is comin' outta my mouth... I'm runnin' and the last time I look back, I trip and I fall... off a building!

I'm fallin' now. The air is beatin' against my opened, button-down shirt like the wind through

a ripped parachute. It's all in slow motion—it's
takin' forever...I keep waitin' for the inevitable,
when I finally hit the street, and all of this'll be
over and done, but death just won't come—not
yet... I try screamin' again, but just like last time
nothin's comin' out, not a sound. I'm prepared for
impact, any moment now. Like a skydiver, I turn
my body over in mid-air. The street below is
gettin' closer and closer, and I think about all of
the people I love—people I'm gonna miss. Then,
as I hit—the street turns into...

Water?!

But, I CAN'T SWIM!! I'm flailin' in the water,
who or whatever was chasin' me doesn't even
matter now because I CAN NOT SWIM! I'm
lookin' around for someone, ANYONE who can
help. I see one, two...no, five people in the water,
and for a minute I think, 'Johnny, you gonna be
alright!' But as I look closer I realize, these boys
ain't movin'. They're all dead, drowned in the
London Avenue Canal over the past few years.
Now I know where I am, and I know what my
chances are. The longer I'm in this water, the
more I begin to realize just how cold this water is,
and the more I fight the water... the heavier my
clothes feel, and...the more...*tired*...I'm gettin'... I
start to...*sink*...

I'm sinkin' now beneath the surface of the water. I'm weak, I'm gaspin' for air, but just like my cryin' out for help, nothin' is comin'. As my consciousness starts to slip in and out, I'm seein' things, like our graduation from St. Matthew's

...My mama and daddy...and Marie...I come back to myself, sinkin', drownin', dyin'... As continue to sink, I start to see stuff floatin' up from the bottom. I feel it brushin' against my hands and arms—real lightly. It's...*money?!*

Bills—20's, 50's, 100's—all floatin' up from the bottom. It gets to the point that the water seems to be filled with money...before I take my last breath...before my lungs fill up...before I black out for good...I can hear Coo Corn Bread whisper...

find that money...

MAN, I HATE NIGHTMARES! I always wake up *after* I'm dead—it's not normal! Everybody I know says they wake up *just before they die*, but not me, noooo... I get to go through every part of the dying process. And when I do wake up, it's always like somebody set off a bomb and I'm soakin' wet, like I just peed in the bed! The sounds from my nightmare—still ringin' in my ears—are louder than anything in the room. Then, just over the sound of the box fan in my window,

I can still hear Coo Corn Bread's voice... *find that money...*

So I found myself at Mark and his brother, Michael's bedroom window, in the back of their seven-room, shotgun house. I was tappin', hopin' Mark would get up first this time, but as usual...

"Man, what do you want?" Michael sleepily asked. "I don't know what time it is, but you definitely don't know what time it is if you at this window, this time 'a night! — Mark? Get up! It's Johnny."

Mark was still rubbin' the 'eye crackers' outta his eyes. "Johnny, you know it's — "

"Mark, I got it... I got a way we can get the money."

"What money?"

"The money for Mr. Willie and Miss Verna..."

"How?"

"Meet me by Danny and Will's in the morning, I'll tell you then."

I was nervous — *really* nervous. The fellas knew I had *some ideas* in the past, but nothin' like this.

109

I knew we wanted to help Mr. Willie and Miss Verna to keep their store. I knew Mr. Willie and Miss Verna's insurance wasn't enough to take care of Mr. Willie's medical bills, and pay for the mortgage while he was getting' better. I knew none of us had the money, and I knew we had to do somethin'.

As I turned the corner of the fence by Danny and Will's house, I could see everybody was there — everybody 'cept Auston. I figured he wouldn't be far behind me. As I stopped at the edge of the steps, everything was silent, they were lookin' for me to say somethin' first. As I started to open my mouth, Auston came up behind me and broke the silence.

"Say Bloodhounds! Okay Johnny, what you got us out here for?"

I never said anything to anybody before now, so I was finally gonna tell 'em all about the night I ran into Coo Corn Bread, and what he told me about the money, Miss Muvalla, and the map. I knew it sounded crazy, but we had to do somethin' to help Mr. Willie and Miss Verna — they loved Back-a-town and *they loved us*...

"Coo-Corn Bread is CRAZY!" said Auston.

"I'm surprised you didn't disappear like they say them other children did! But you gonna let a CRAZY MAN make you think there's some map out there that's gonna lead us to a bunch a money?! YOU CRAZY TOO!"

"Whoa, wait na' Auston..." said Big Ed, Jr. "...maybe... maybe he was tellin' the truth..."

"...and maybe pigs fly, Ed!"

Try 'na calm Auston down, Mark said, "But c'mon Auston, we gotta do somethin' for Mr. Willie and Miss Verna..."

"What else can we do? We don't have much time...," said Will.

Even though most of the time Auston was a hot-head, he had his more "practical" moments. "Have y'all forgotten 'where' this place is?!"

I knew it was gonna take some convincin' to get Auston down with the plan. It involved goin' to the French Quarter, which we were never allowed to go to without our parents or some adult from the family. That's just how it was. But we weren't goin' just any place in the French Quarter. We were gonna have to go *into* a **voodoo shop!**

All of us, whether Baptist or Catholic, were church goin' folks. Church goin' folks didn't do no voodoo shops. There were some things Black parents just didn't play with — voodoo was at the top of the list!

"...you know how much Mr. Willie and Miss Verna need that money, Auston..."

"But Danny — I..."

Auston could begin to see, everybody else didn't care how crazy the whole thing sounded. This was about helpin' Mr. Willie and Miss Verna. You could tell he was strugglin' with it, goin' back and forth in his mind about it.

"...and if we can get it for 'em, we'll save the store." I said.

"...and maybe help pay some of Mr. Willie's hospital bills," Said Mark.

You could always tell when Auston finally made a decision to do somethin' crazy — he'd always get this funny, cheese-eatin' grin on his face. So, finally, he gave in.

"Awright... When do we make our move?"

We walked down Duels Street to Pauger. As we turned right and walked down two blocks, our minds began to shift toward what we would have to do. We'd never gone to the Quarter without our parents and NEVER gone to a voodoo shop. Nobody said a word as we turned left, and headed down three more blocks to the Elysian Fields bus stop. Big Ed, Jr. broke the silence.

"What if we don't find the map?

It was as if nobody had ever considered this as a possibility. I mean, we were talkin' about a map that NO ONE had ever seen. This was a huge risk...especially if our folks found out. I was all set to say somethin' smart back to Ed, 'cuz I thought saying anything that would cause us to doubt ourselves was the last thing anybody needed to hear—but just then, the bus pulled up.

Even though it took forever to get down there, it didn't even matter. We had our minds set on makin' things right for Mr. Willie and Miss Verna.

Finally, we arrived in the French Quarter. Anxious to get there, we all piled out the back of the bus, and ran down Decatur Street and crossed over Esplanade Avenue. The first thing that got us was the smell!

"Daaaaaanngg! Does it ALWAYS smell like this down here?!"

Big Ed, Jr. was holdin' his nose while he talked. And he wasn't kiddin! It was the first time we had been down there without their parents, and it must've been garbage day, 'cuz you could smell it waaaaaayyy before you saw it. There was still the smell of all of the parties that must've gone on the night before — all 'the beer bottles, and paper trash, and narrow alley ways where guys must've relieved themselves, 'cuz they couldn't find a toilet. The combination of those smells could open up the most congested nose!

We still had a way to go before we got to Muvalla's, which was in a part of the quarter where locals normally wouldn't take their kids. Like I said before, our folks put the fear of God in us about goin' to the French Quarter, and bein' that Auston's daddy was a deacon at The Greater Mt. Zion Missionary Baptist Church, they'd kill us if they found out we were in some voodoo shop... so we had to make sure they would never find out...

As we made our way through the narrow streets, we came to an old, grey one-story shotgun/camel-back house with stone steps and a short porch. It would look like any other French Quarter building... 'Cept this one had an eerie sense of "death."

114

You didn't know if the shape of the place was just for show, or if she really didn't take care of it... it looked BAD... The ancient, wind-worn sign had fresh paint on the lettering: MADAME MUVALLA'S VOODOO EMPORIUM. After all of our talk, nobody was willin' to open the door, so Will said,

"So... we here now..."

"Yeah..." said Danny. "Who's goin' in first?"

"Na--not me..." Ed stuttered. "I ain't goin' in there first, no..."

"What, you scary?"

"Y'all stop it...stop it Auston!" I said... "It's just a shop..." But nothin' I said at that moment was gonna stop the guys from thinkin' out loud.

"Yeah, a voodoo shop..."

"Yeah, a big voodoo shop..."

Finally, Mark got us back on track. "And what's that Will?"

"I...I don't know..."

"Well that's just it, c'mon Bloodhounds..."

I reached for the doorknob and as the door opened, we all jumped because of an old bell mounted on the back of the door, that didn't start to ring until after the door really got goin'. Inside, the smell seemed to steal any remainin' fresh air we brought with us from outside. There was the faint smell of mold in the air—mold and cigarettes—Kool's.

The house looked as if it was packed from the front room to the back, filled with "voodoo" stuff— "gris gris," the lil' voodoo necklaces; historic facts and fables about New Orleans, voodoo and the French Quarter; wax figures of infamous voodoo personalities, like Marie Laveaux; and maps—lots of maps.

"Bloodhounds, let's spread out, look around and see if any of the maps got St. Christopher's Marsh on it—but, BE QUIET…"

Silently, we moved between the tall, dark brown bookshelves and around the glass cases spread around the first two rooms of the shop. Nobody said a word until…

"Something you look for?"

We all could'a jumped out of our skins! We all looked up at the same time. At the back of the second room, from behind a doubled curtain hung in the doorway stood, a short, stout, dark woman with a patois-like accent. We were all still frozen in our tracks when she asked,

"...something you seek?"

She was starin' all of us down at one time! Then, a slow, sinister grin spread across her twisted face. Madame Muvalla... What folks said about her was true... She was alive alright, but she really looked like a dead woman... Her skin was real dark and shiny...like one'a them dead bodies Mark and I used to serve funerals over... As she moved closer to us, everybody started backin' away — everybody but Mark and me.

"Do you fear me?"

"Na---No...No I ain't scared..." Even though my voice was shakin' a little, I wasn't gonna move... no backin' down...And it was workin' too, 'cuz she kinda backed up, and changed her tone.

"Good... No scary boys need come 'ere...have you come for a 'tour'?"

She turned away from us, acting as if she was attending to her shelves. The rest of the Bloodhounds, still speechless, were just noddin' their heads, while Mark and I talked to her.

"No, we wanna know if you got a map..."

Madame Muvalla turned back toward Mark.

"A 'map' you say?"

The rest of the Bloodhounds nodded their heads.

"I sell many, many maps, to many, many places... plantations, Marie Laveaux's grave site, haunted mansions... Where is it you desire to go?"

"We lookin' for a treasure map..." I said. Once the word, 'map' was spoken, the rest of the guys started to loosen up.

"Yeah," said Will. "...a map to where they got millions a dollars hidden!"

Muvalla drew up a long, slow, growling kind of laugh, almost like an old man.

...A "treasure" map? What... you got a ship to sail to some far -away island?

The rest of the Bloodhounds were lookin' at Muvalla and then at me, try'na size up the situation. Were they led on a wild goose chase? Or, is there more to this? Mark made it plain:

"No lady... We heard you had some kind 'a map to where some money was hid."

"And why do you think I would just be holdin' this...map?"

Her words seemed to just hang in the air over us, like a big tree gettin' ready to fall on all of us. We were all stunned... It might sound stupid, but we never... I never considered *that* question. So, I tried to make sense of the situation while she did the talkin'.

"...don't you think I would use the map and get the money for myself?"

I felt like interrogatin' her — I wasn't about to just turn around now.

"So... you tellin' us you never heard 'a no map before... We jus' came down here for nuthin?"

"I'm afraid so, chere... Ya' see, "if" there was a map out there, with money like you say there is, then nothin' would stop Muvalla from goin' out and findin' it, ya' hear?"

We all had the look of total defeat in our eyes; I was no exception. I looked around; heads started to hang low. Then, as if she had us at the edge of a cliff, and needed just one little push to send us over the side,

"...but, if it's other maps to other wonderful, mysterious locations in New Orleans and the surroundin' areas, you let me know..."

Just then, Muvalla's assistant, a lil' man who looked like he slept in his clothes, came in from smoking a cigarette out back. Muvalla addressed him, and the Bloodhounds, before taking her leave of us.

"Miles," she said in an authoritative voice, "the boys can look around a bit more if they'd like... I have an errand to run, and will be back shortly... Take care young boys... In spite of its futility, I hope someday, you will find what it is you're lookin' for...eventually..."

Muvalla swept aside the curtain in the doorway, and disappeared. A minute later, you could hear what must've been the back door shut. The Bloodhounds stood speechless, in the center of the first room in the shop. It was like getting' sucker-punched in the stomach. Auston was the first one to catch his breath.

"So... This is what we came out here for? ...this is what we risked gettin' our behinds beat for?"

"Aw Auston stop..." said Will.

"STOP WHAT?! We came out here fo' NUTHIN!"

"I don't know what to say..."

"Don't say nuthin' Johnny, just SHUT UP!"

Mark had heard enough from Auston.

"Auston, I'm gettin' tired of you..."

"TIRED OF WHAT MARK? YOU WANNA FIGHT OR SOMETHIN'?!"

While most of us had our attention turned toward Auston and Mark, Big Ed, Jr. had wandered off into the rear of the shop, behind the same curtain Muvalla made her exit. He started lookin' at voodoo dolls, fake chickens, all kinds of "tourist" voodoo stuff.

Big Ed, forgot that his Aunt Mercedes used to call him "bull in a china closet." He ran into a huge painting of a voodoo ceremony, and then backed into a shelf, filled with stuff. Both the shelf and everything on it came crashing down on his head.

BAM! ...BLAM!... BAM!!!

We heard the commotion from the next room. I snapped outta my disappointment over the map. Auston and Mark forget about their feud, and when we all ran into the next room we found him…

Big Ed, Jr. was buried under a mountain of books, trinkets, talismans, and other "voodoo paraphernalia." Miles and the rest of us started to dig him out.

"What were you doin back here?!" Miles said.

"I…I was jus' lookin..."

"You could'a killed yourself back here boy!" said Auston.

"Yeah, you could'a' got yourself hurt real bad..."

"You awright son?" said Miles.

"Yeah... I guess so..."

"Good, 'cuz we ain't got no in-surance for accidents like this..." Miles scoffed. "…and if you break anything-a-Miss Muvalla's, you buy it!"

"Mister, HE ain't got no money!" Will announced.

We all fell out laughin', except Big Ed, Jr., of course—he failed to see the humor in it.

"I *do* have money... What you talkin' 'bout?"

We helped Miles pick up the rest of the merchandise. Just then, Will noticed a corner of paper sticking out from an old, pewter jewelry box. He pulled the corner out from the box, and unfolded the paper, revealing what looked like an old, yellowed...

MAP...

"Hey... I....I FOUND A MAP!"

"A WHAT?!"

"A MAP, AUSTON!"

"Naw, it can't be..."

I knew better.

"I bet it IS!"

Everybody else was more skeptical, but I felt a sense of hope again. The thing was, to find out whether this was just any old "map," or the map we'd been lookin' for. With Muvalla still out on her errands, we started to grill Miles for more information.

"So, just what is this map?"

"I dunno..." said Miles. "It don't look like the ones we usually sell around here..."

"Well, how much you want for it?" I was on a mission.

He gave absolutely no thought to it.

"I dunno, a buck?"

"ONE DOLLAR?!"

He looked at us, real irritated.

"Ohhh… if that's "too much" well..."
"NO, NO a buck is fine..." I said.

I reached into my pocket, pulling out a dollar from the roll of money we'd collected around Back-a-town.

"…a buck is just fine..."

Miles must've picked up on our enthusiasm and was startin' to wonder if the buck was a good deal.

"What y'all need a map for anyhow?"

I wasn't gonna lie.

"We heard there was a map leadin' to millions a dollars buried somewhere..."

"Oh… you mean from that robbery?"

Time stopped… we all looked at each other in amazement. This was the first time anyone had, even in part, backed up Coo-Corn Bread's story… still; I tried to play it off.

"Yeah... Yeah that's the one..."

"Well, I wouldn't say that's the map or anything..." Miles said. "…far as I know, the story about it is more fiction than fact..."

Then Mark started in on 'im.

"So, what happened mister?"

As Miles told the story, it was as if we were right there.

"Well, folks say there was a robbery back in '66. Y'all were prob'ly too young to remember it...there were these three guys, dressed in nice suits, with hats and overcoats... Kinda like Elliott Ness and the Untouchables... 'cept these were bad guys, on a mission. They were out to hit the bank before the business day got too busy... It happened on a Friday, and folks say there were

125

some people in the bank at the time... They say one of 'em did all the talkin'

"LADIES AND GENTLEMEN THIS IS A STICK-UP! THIS IS NOT A DRILL! EVERYBODY PUT YOUR HANDS UP!"

As Miles continued, we all stood there, fixed on his every word.

"...they stuck the place up, made off with the goods... Some estimated the take to be around fifteen million dollars..."

FIFTEEN MILLION DOLLARS?! I couldn't get that number outta' my head.

"...the three robbers all sat in an old warehouse, at an office table, rejoicing over their new-found wealth. All around them are stacks-a-20's and 50's and100 dollar bills, money bands and the bags. But, in the middle of their celebration, four more men entered the room...they got somethin' they never bargained for...the double-cross..."

It was as if the whole room held its breath at the same time... Miles paused, still thinkin' on the details of the story...then he continued.

"...some Folks say it was the guards from the armored car that done it...but we really don't know... ya' see, nobody ever saw them guards after the robbery..."

"So..." Danny cut in. "...why do people say there's some kinds map then?"

"I dunno... Some folks claim the guards got found out, and tried to hide in the St. Christopher's marshlands, somewhere out there in the east..."

"One story is that, they decided to bury the money out there, until things cooled down, so they probably had to make a map to figure out how to get back to where they hid it...but no one knows fo' sure..."

"A lot's been said about that robbery, and what people think happened to the guards and to the money... Some folks believe them boys is livin' it up somewhere in some foreign country, or in the islands somewhere..."

"Since the bank was insured, everybody who had money in there got their money back... So, I guess people kind 'a forgot about it after-while... Ya' only hear about that story every once in a while..."

Big Ed, Jr. got up from where he was sittin' on the floor and walked toward Miles.

"So, what you think Mr. Miles? 'You think that money's still out there?"

Miles shrugged, "Humph... I... I dunno what to think... I mean, it could be, but then again maybe not..."

"You think this map is it?" I asked.

Miles just fell out laughin'. He started coughin' then snot comin' outta his nose— He must've laughed for 5 minutes straight, almost fallin' over himself on the floor. I didn't see anything funny 'bout my question. Finally, he got himself together...

"If it was *the map*, do you think for one minute that I would *sell it to you for a dollar*?

He made a lotta sense... Still, I had a feelin' there was somethin' to our hearin' 'bout this map and this story...

But I just played it off...

"No... No I guess not... BLOODHOUNDS?"

We all got up off the floor and headed for the front door. Like I said, if this was the map, the last thing we needed to do was *act like it.*

"Thanks mister..." I said politely. "We appreciate you sellin' us the map and the story and all... But, we gotta get back to Back-a-town."

"Okay, no problem... "He says. "But, what's this Bloodhounds thing?"

Danny, Will, and I answered his question in succession

"Oh, we the Bloodhounds..."

"..from Back-a-town..."

"...and Bloodhounds from Back-a-town DON'T BACK DOWN!

We all made our way out of the door, some walking forward, others backing out to wave at Miles as we left. We were walking on air, givin' each other "dap" and jumpin' up and down when we heard a dog barking and it getting louder by the second.

POOCHIE?!!

It was Danny and Will's dog, Poochie...Here we were, miles from home, and this dog managed to find us AGAIN...

"Dang fellas!" says Auston. "That dog is always followin' us!

"Why y'all don't put him on a leash?"

"Shut up Auston," Danny came back at 'im. "… you know he always chews through 'em."

"…yeah Aus," said Ed, "it's not his fault, he just wants to be free, ya' know?"

We all looked at Big Ed, Jr. —like he lost his mind…

"What?"He said.

"C'mon fellas…" I said. "We need to be gettin' back home… We got a lot a work to do and not a lot a time…"

We all started toward home, when all of a sudden, Poochie sat down on the side of the curb. Will noticed first.

"Poochie…c'mon boy…"

"What's wrong with that dog?" whined Auston. "…he follows us all the way here, now he wants to jus' sit down?"

Danny ran over to the curb to get'im… somethin' 'bout that dog… it was always like, he knew somethin' we didn't.

"C'mon Poochie, we gotta go NOW..."

Danny grabbed Poochie by the collar, and pulled him along, until he started to walk behind us. Poochie walked for a little while then paused again, looking back toward the shop.

"POOCHIE!"

Just after we left the shop, Madame Muvalla must've come back from her errands.

"Miles... 'dem boys left I see?"

"Yeah," Miles grunted. "...just a minute ago."

Muvalla's face contorted, like she was try'na add up the time she'd been gone and, figuring we should'a left long before this.

"They *just* left?"

"Yeah, they stuck around a while, just talkin'... Anyways, I gotta' get lunch now. I'm goin' get a po-boy-- you want somethin'?"

"No..." She paused. "...wait, maybe some Pall Mall's."

Miles nodded his head, and left. Muvalla stood in the doorway between the main room and the adjacent room, when a hand reached up from behind, and covered her mouth. She tried to struggle to free herself, to scream, but couldn't. She probably thought this was it… somebody she'd swindled in the past finally caught up with her…

"You stop strugglin' and maybe I'll let'cha go…"

She knew that voice… a single tear ran down the side of her cheek…

She knew that voice…gruff…terrifyin' to enemies, but to a friend… to a long-lost love…

Her whole body relaxed and so did the hand over her mouth. She pulled the hand down a little from her mouth and whispered,

"Morris?"

She turned around and started to hug and squeeze him until he could hardly breathe.

"Whoa na' hold on girl, you gon' kill me if ya' keep squeezin' me that way…"

"I…I can't believe you're… here! Here with me, finally after all this time… What it's been… Almost ten years?"

"Ten years, three months, six days, twenty-one hours, thirty-three minutes aaaand… fifteen seconds."

Ex-cons always knew how ta' tell time, based on the last time they were free. Morris was no exception. Folks said he'd been and done a lotta stuff over his life…'that he was smart, but always had his mind set on evil.

"Ya' drunk, hunh?" Muvalla could tell by the smell.

"No, baby… jus' a lil' bit tipsy is all… How you doin'?"

"Fine… after all them years in prison, ya' come back to me, lookin' like you in good spirits… or is it just the bottle?"

"No gurl…" Morris was smooth. "…I'm happy as hell! I come up here 'cuz I came back for what's mine, and to keep my promise to pay you for helpin' me…"

"Yours? …Oh, you mean the map?"

"You know it… It's time, Val… time for me--for us to get what we so richly deserve… Me--for bein' patient all these years and you… For bein' a good lil' safety deposit box and for keepin' yo' mouth shut…"

Morris went back into the adjacent room, looking around the shop in the section where an old, pewter jewelry box was, a jewelry box with a map in it. Muvalla stayed in the main shop area, still day-dreamin' about being reunited with Morris.

"...from what I remember Val, that money is out there in the marshes...after Chef Menteur Highway... 'Boo-key,' the map gives landmarks to its exact location... Didn't you say you put it in some jewelry box?"

Muvalla started to come outta her trance, "Yeah, a pewter jewelry box, why?"

"It ain't here..."

She froze... her legs got weak...

"What did you say?"

"You heard me woman, IT AIN'T IN HERE!"

Morris started pullin' everything off of every shelf in the place. Drawers are pulled out and flipped upside down... still...

Nothin'...

"Hey Miss Muvalla I got you that pack of..."

In one, fluid motion, Morris jumped on Miles, drove him into one wall of the shop, as more voodoo dolls crashed to the floor.

"WHERE IS IT?!" Morris growled like a wild animal or somethin' — he had a long, silver blade under Miles' throat...

"It?! Wha... WHAT ARE YOU TALKIN' 'BOUT MAN?!"

"THE MAP! THE DAMN MAP! WHERE'S MY MAP?!"

"WWWHA...WHAT MAP?!"

"THE MAP I LEFT IN THE BOTTOM OF THIS JEWELRY BOX, FOOL! What did you do with it — YOU TRY'NA KEEP IT FOR YOURSELF?"

It's funny...not in a laughin' kinda' way...how a man sometimes'll say somethin' *really stupid*, in hopes that it'll save his life... Miles was one a' those men and this was one a' those times...

"NO...NO, I sold it...today... to some kids...

"You *SOLD IT*...to *SOME KIDS*?!"

Morris let Miles go for a moment, but grew more furious with every moment as Miles still tried to explain himself.

"Yeah, some kids came in here, knocked over the bookshelf, and it broke open... They found the map in the bottom of the jewelry box...I...I Didn't know it was important to you — to anybody...they were just a bunch of kids from Back-a-town... So, I sold it to 'em...

"Back-a-town," coughed Morris. "...how do you know that?"

"cuz they said so, I heard 'em talkin' 'bout bein' from there."

"How much... How much did *you* sell it for?!"

"A... dollar..."

Can you imagine what must've been goin' through Morris' half-drunk all-twisted mind? Here ya' got millions of dollars jus' waitin' for ya' to come and pick up, and ride off into the sunset...when along comes some "feck" who sells ya' dream, ya' promise, YOUR HOPE...

For a buck...

"A dollar?! YOU SOLD IT FOR ONE DOLLAR?!"

Morris threw Miles back against the wall.

"Do you know what you've done? That map's got the location of OVER 15 MILLION DOLLARS IN CASH! And you SOLD IT to some KIDS FOR ONE DOLLAR?!!"

"I... I... UMMMPH"

Any further explanation from Miles was interrupted...

Permanently...

Morris ran' Miles through with that long knife...holding the knife in with one hand and holdin' Miles' mouth closed with the other, until his last breath left his body. Madame Muvalla, there the entire time, was paralyzed with fear. If Morris was drunk before, he was straight-sober now... back in top, killin' form. With nothin' to lose, he would stop at nothing to get what he wanted.

As he let Miles' body slowly slump into a pile on the floor, he spoke to the only livin' witness in the room.

"...now look ol' woman... seein' as though we' in this together now... I suggest you find a way that 'you' can get rid of this body, and then help me...

find *them kids..."*

CHAPTER 5

After comin' back from the French Quarter, we stopped at Auston's. We finally had the map, but there was just one problem...

None of us could read it...

As usual, Auston was the first one to be *positive* about our current situation.

"I know we' all supposed to be BOY SCOUTS and all but, CAN ANY OF *YOU* READ A MAP?!"

"Of course," I said, "...we can read it, right guys?"

At first, we were about as confident that somebody could read that map, as we were that the Saints were gonna win the Super Bowl that year.

Just so ya' know, that year *the Saints were 4 and 11*...

"I mean look... It looks so *general*," said Auston.

139

"No, look man," I said. "... There's where the marsh starts..."

"Yeah, right off Chef Highway..." said Will.

"...and that's where it looks like... Hey, where do we start once we get to the marsh?"

Mark kinda' summed it up.

"...yeah, it does look like a general map of the east... nuthin' special 'bout it...what'chu think Johnny?"

"...well, they always say maps like this have hidden clues..."

"...AND?"

"AND, we just gotta find the clues..."

"But what clues Johnny," said Big Ed, Jr. "it...it Just looks like a regular map is all..."

Danny agreed, "He's right Johnny... I don't see no..."

I didn't let'em finish...no time to argue about it... I did what anybody who ever read a mystery novel did...

I put a match to it...

"JOHNNY! STOP! YOU GONNA BURN IT!"

Mark grabbed Auston... he read those novels too...

"Hold up man... He knows what he's doin'..."

As I held the flame under the map, words begin to appear in the section of the map that forms the Lake Pontchatrain. Slowly, words started to appear from the flame. The words were written in ink that only became visible by heat. I moved the flame from side-to-side behind the map until the match burned my fingers. When I finished, the words became clear to everybody...

"...four Miles more north from Water's edge, turn left at yonder oak; 100 paces onward and, remember not to choke; your silent guide in moss is clad, His finger points the way; and to two more like him just as bad, have even less to say; but when you've found the last of them, while mute yet still they speak; their final gesture leads the way to all that which you seek..."

Now, we had somethin'.

"Bloodhounds, we just found our first clue...now, we need a plan...let's all get together in 30..."

We all met back at the usual place, Danny and Will's house, and began to work out our plan... We didn't have much time, because St. Christopher's Marsh was a long way off... We'd have to catch the Broad bus to the end of the line, and walk the rest of the way just to get to the edge of the marsh... Then we'd have to find the clues from the map...we'd have to find the money, and get back home before our folks found out... But to do all that...

...we'd have to lie...A LOT...

We'd all have to give the same "story" to our parents. We were all gonna go swimmin' at the pool, and NORD was holdin' its 10th Annual Summer Baseball Tournament at Hardin Park...

Cars, station wagons, and vans full a' NORD baseball players and their parents would close in on the park. Plus all the people comin' to swim...there'd be so many people out at Hardin from all over New Orleans, not even our folks would try to look for us out there...and besides, all our daddy's were gonna be workin' on Saturday, so they wouldn't be out there to check on us.

We'd all needed about $5.00 in change — enough for each of us to pay the 40 cents bus fare each way... We'd have to travel about 13 miles to get to St. Christopher's, and at least another 3 to 4

miles north, into the marsh. The only road goin'
out there was Chef Menteur Highway... we could
catch the Broad bus as far as it went to Village de
L'est (the east village), and walk the rest of the
way.

We would need our pack/frames to carry the
money with... since all of us were in the boy
scouts, and we been hikin' before, that wasn't the
problem... but the trick was, gettin' our stuff out
of the closets without lookin' crazy to our
parents... and gettin' away from our houses
without bein' noticed... I mean, six guys with
camping equipment looks kind'a "crazah" if you
s'posed to be goin' watch a baseball
tournament...so we'd tell them we needed the
packs to put our swimmin' trunks and towels in.

So the next day, all the NORD baseball teams
we used to play — Conrad, Bunny Friend,
Shakespeare, Milne, Rosenwald, Harrell, even
Lyons Center came to Hardin baseball field.
Umpires and coaches mingled with each other
while the parents and fans shouted support for,
and trash against, each other's teams.

We would act like we were gonna be there all
day, and since the games started at 8:00 in the
morning, and final game wouldn't be 'til at least
8:00 that night, we figured we'd have enough
time to get out to the east and back before our
anybody would catch us...

Myron West was one of the baseball players from Hardin's 12 and 13-year-old team, but the way he acted, you'da never thought he was from Back-a-town. He didn't like us (he especially didn't like Auston), an' we fo'sure didn't like him. He was lookin' at us now with our backpacks…probably wonderin' what we were doin' with backpacks at a baseball park.

"Hey w'us up y'all?"

"Nuthin' Myron, w'us up with you?"

"'Jus warmin' up… gettin' ready to beat up on Rosenwald… 'them boy's is soft… where y'all goin?"

"Nunya," Auston said…

"Nunya?"

"Nunya bizzness…"

We all bust out laughin'. Auston had good timin' on that one, but Myron was not amused. With bat in hand, he turned to face Auston, who wasn't about to back down. Myron got in his face.

"Say boy, ya' better watch ya' mouth… Ol' high-low-hickey-head…"

"Who you callin' high-low-hickey-head... Ol'
slap-back-head, bench warmin'..."

"Say Aus," I cut right between 'em, "...that's
enough...we goin' swim first, then we gonna
watch y'all play... 'you think y'all gonna get to
the finals tonight, Myron?"

"What'chu say boy, we got the whip!"

"Awright Myron, we gonna see..."

Myron turned away from us, swinging his bat
like he thought he was Hank Aaron or somethin'.
Auston had to get the last word.

"...Ol' Slap-back-head..."

"C'mon Aus, stop it..."

"That boy's a feck and y'all know it!"

Yeah," said Ed, "... but he IS on the team..."

"What?" Auston said... all defensive... "I
could'a made the team... if I wanted to..."

Now THAT was funny. But Auston was serious.

"...I Just didn't wanna practice all spring and
summer that's all..."

Danny fell out on the ground and we all busted out laughin'

"YOU WHAT?!!"

"Auston," Will was still bent over laughin', "...if it ain't a football, YOU CAN'T CATCH IT!"

"He's right, he's right," said Ed."

"...and if it ain't bigger than a basketball, YOU KNOW YOU CAN'T HIT IT!"

Auston just stood there, while we rolled around on the ground laughin'. He knew we were right, that boy was S-A-D, SAD!

"Man y'all wrong for that, yeah..."

We made good on lookin' like we were havin' fun at the pool and the game, but now it was time for the Bloodhounds to make our break from the park, and get to St. Christopher's marsh.

"We know what we got to do, right Bloodhounds?"

"YEAH..."

"We ready?"

"You know we are Johnny," said Mark.

So we left the park, one by one, through that big hole in the back fence on the North Dorgenois Street side of the park. We all got out, and headed for London Avenue. We were on our way...

And we were bein' followed...

The drainpipe...

Here I was again, at the drainpipe. The stakes this time though, were a whole lot higher than braggin' rights behind a football game. I never liked that drainpipe... I never liked that canal...

But, as usual, Danny and Will made it look easy; runnin' across the length of the pipe...Auston and Mark followed...even Big Ed, Jr., as big as he was... still made it over pretty fast...just like his daddy...walkin' cross them roofs and bein' that big...

The rest of the Bloodhounds were jumping up and down, waving me on, like as if I was roundin' third base, for home plate.

But... I just stood there...lookin...

"C'mon Johnny! You can do it!"

In my mind I could see them nightmares I used to have...falling off buildings and drowning. But this time, I started seein' Mr. Willie and Miss Verna, the map and the money.

...so today, for me... was gonna be *different*...

...today, I was gonna master this thing...

I started to "walk" across the drainpipe, arms extended out to the sides...one foot in front of the other...

Perfect balance...

I couldn't hear nothin'... no wind, no cars, no voices, nothin'...'til I reached the other side...

YEAAAAAAAHHHH!!!!

The bloodhounds shouted! They kept givin' me dap, givin' each other dap, and jumpin' up and down.

I got through it...

I got over it...

Fifteen minutes later, we were at the Broad Bus stop, at Broad and St. Anthony. By my watch, the next Broad-Village de L'est bus would get to us in twenty minutes. All we had to do was wait and not get noticed by anyone...

"DANG!"

"Well, if it ain't them, Back-a-town fecks..."

Of all of the people we DIDN'T need to see, Larry
and Randy were at the top of the list. They had
big mouths, and they were bound to tell
somebody that they saw us and what we were
doin'

"Y'all a lil' far from Back-a-town right now,
huh Johnny?"

"We got other business to tend to."

"BIZNESS? Oh, so fecks like you got *bizness*?

Mark tried to smooth things a bit. "Yeah, we goin'
campin' Larry... You know, like boy scouts?"

"Stop try'na be smart, fool..." Randy snapped
back.

"Well tell ya' boy not to be so stupid," said
Will.

Larry started to move toward Will, but I cut him
off.

"Y'all boys gotta have somethin' better to do
than to try to mess with us..."

"Yeah," said Auston, "...like gettin' ya' behind whipped by "Bill Dirt" and 'em boys from Vascoville..."

Larry and Randy froze in their tracks. For once Auston knew how to pull their card... He found out that Larry and his boys got skull-dragged by Billy Whitehouse and his boys from Vascoville, behind Dillard. Folks used to call him "Billy-Dirt," 'cuz they say he always looked like he was dirty...

"...yeah, y'all didn't think we'd find out... My cousin is from Vascoville and EV'RYBODY over there know..."

Larry and Randy started to backin' up. They'd been found out.

"Y'all ain't so bad now, huh?"

"Y'all still can't whip us, Johnny" Larry cried.

"Yeah, well let's see...we can always meet up at Dillard again... next Saturday sound good to you?

"Y....yeah, Sure... We gonna still whip y'all!"

I walked right up to Larry Charbonnet, nose-to-nose...I had just finished walkin' across a drainpipe where a bunch-a-kids drowned... dealing with Larry was *easy*.

"I...wouldn't be so sure about that, PODNUH..."

Just then, the Broad-Village de L'est bus arrived, doors open. Most of the BLOODHOUNDS get on board, but I waited 'til last

"Y'all take care, Larry...Randy... and stay outta Vascoville...word is, y'all don't do your best work there..."

We all bust out laughin' as the bus pulls off, leaving Larry and Randy looking at each other, like they was stupid or somethin'. Larry and Randy were still by the bus top when a car pulled up.

"Say," said the man from inside the car, "...you boys from 'round here?"

"What's it look like to you, man?" Larry came back at 'im.

Just as Larry started to say somethin' else smart, the man in the car pulled out a long...big-barreled pistol, pointed it through his window at them, and cocked it.

"Ya' people never told you respect your elders?"

Larry and Randy were frozen solid. Then, they say Randy broke out runnin' and left Larry standin' there… still frozen by the sight of the pistol…

"I… I…"

"Now, I asked you a question, boy… *are you from 'round here?*"

Larry could only nod his head.

"That's better… now… you know anything 'bout some boys call themselves, "The Bloodhounds?"

Larry nodded his head again, as a single tear ran down his cheek.

Meanwhile, The Bloodhounds were all seated at the back of the bus. We were full of nervous excitement, and anticipation, but we were in for a long ride. The bus was a local, and would stop just about every two or three blocks.

A long bus ride always made folks hungry, and Big Ed, Jr. was no exception.

"I'm hungry…

"Well Ed," said Auston, "…eat somethin' then."

"Oh yeah..."

Big Ed, Jr. opened up his pack, and pulled out a extra-large bag of Cajun Craw-tater Zapp's he'd packed earlier.

"I get hungry when I'm excited."

"Well, you must STAY excited, 'cuz you STAY EATIN', YEAH!"

"Oh you funny now, huh Danny?"

DANNY laughed, and laughed, while Will and Mark just shook their heads.

"Johnny," said Ed, "... after 'we find this money...after we take care of Mr. Willie and Miss Verna and all...we' gonna have a lotta' money left over...what we gonna do with it?

I didn't know what to say... I spent so much time thinkin' about Mr. Willie and Miss Verna...all of us did... that I never thought about *us havin' money left over.*

"I dunno Ed... I...I might just give it away..."

"I know you crazy bruh!"

"No, Auston, I'm serious..."

"Yeah, you gotta be crazy... I get money...I'm gonna spend it on things..."

"What kind of things?" said Mark.

"I dunno Mark... things for me... things I always wanted.

"Aus, you never thought about doin' somethin' nice for somebody else?"

"No, that's not it...I mean; I'd give money to my church and all... You know, tithe and offerings, like my mama and daddy do... and I'd give money to other people who need stuff..."

"...like Coo-Corn Bread?"

Auston paused. Coo-Corn Bread was a perfect example of somebody who at one time gave his all in life, but who life hadn't been to fair to in return. So for Auston, the answer was simple.

"...yeah...like Coo-Corn Bread...but I would get some stuff for me too..."

"What about you Danny?" said Ed.

"...I would help out my mama and daddy, help them build a bigger house."

"Watch it now Danny, you beginnin' to sound like brother Will..."

"...and what's wrong with soundin' like me?"

"Nuthin' Will," Danny said, "nuthin'..."

Big Ed, Jr. always had a big heart too. As he started, others joined in.

'I would help people who needed their roof fixed, or their house fixed... I would use some of my money for that..."

"Yeah that's good... I would help coach get more uniforms for Hardin Park..."

That got a big laugh from all of us. See, so many of those uniforms had been stolen...ev'rything was miss-match

...they **could** use some *new uniforms*...

CHAPTER 6

The bus has finally reached the end of the line. We were the last to get off, through the rear entrance of the bus. The bus pulled off. All the talkin' and jokin' came to a stop. The dream was now real, and seein' it pull off was a sign that from here on it is on us.

"Aw'right Bloodhounds... This is where we start..."

I pulled out the map, and everything I couldn't remember about map readin' after we'd left Madame Muvalla's started comin' back to me.

"...we gotta hike about 2-3 more miles to hike before we get to the edge of St. Christopher's Marsh."

Big Ed, Jr., Auston, and Will shaded their eyes as they looked up at the hot, Louisiana summer sun.

"...it's already hot out here... 'figure it's gonna get a lot hotter before we reach the marsh... y'all ready?"

They all nodded their heads in affirmation.

"...then let's go..."

As we started walkin' the summer heat started to beat down on us. It was like a thick blanket that was crazy-glued to your skin — you just could not shake off. And our state bird — not the brown pelican, but the "culex" mosquito, made sure we had a proper escort into the marsh. We got off Chef, onto some old access road that nobody seemed to use anymore. I figured it would get us to the marsh faster. And not long after we started, the heat, the humidity, and the mosquitos got us to start draggin'. It was time to pick up the pace...so I started singin' cadence...

"I don't know what you been told..."

"I don't know what you been told..."

"Us Bloodhounds are bad and bold..."

"Us Bloodhounds are bad and bold..."

"Knowin' what we got to do..."

"Knowin' what we got to do..."

"Rep-re-sent troop thir-ty-two..."

"Rep-re-sent troop thir-ty-two..."
"Sound Off!"

"1, 2..."

"Sound off!"

"3, 4..."

"Bring it on down..."

"1, 2, 3, 4... 1, 2... 3, 4!!!"

Mark took point next, and took over the cadence.

"I been east and I been west..."

"I been east and I been west..."

"Bloodhounds, Bloodhounds are the best..."

"Bloodhounds, Bloodhounds are the best..."

"Workin' workin' day and night..."

"Workin' workin' day and night..."

"Ain't gon' stop 'til all is right..."

"Ain't gon' stop 'til all is right..."

"Sound Off!"

"1, 2..."

"Sound off!"

"3, 4..."

"Bring it on down..."

"1, 2, 3, 4... 1, 2... 3, 4!!!"

Big Ed, Jr. was next up...we didn't know what to expect from him. He was outta breath, but jumped right into step with the rest of us.

"Your left... Your left... Your left, right, left..."

"Your left... Your left... Your left, right, left..."

"Your left... Your left... Your left, right, left..."

"Your left... Your left... Your left, right, left..."

"My back is achin'!"

"my drawers too tight!"

"my booty shakin'!"

"from left to right!"

From the back of the formation, Danny cut the cadence off. We all came to a stop.
"NO! NO! That's not it."

"Not it?!" said Ed, "Wha— you got somethin' better?!"

Danny peeled back his shoulders, cupped his hands around his mouth, kicked his head back and yelled...

"INDIANS!"

We didn't get it at first...

"I said, INDIANS!"

The call for "INDIANS" was a call-out in the spirit of the Mardi Gras Indians. All over New Orleans, groups of Mardi Gras Indian "gangs" would assemble in their best costumes and challenge each other with chants, dances, and songs. It was as basic to our culture as bein' Black... So, the call-out was kind-a-like a call to arms... For the Bloodhounds it was a call to pick up the pace and get to St. Christopher's marsh. So, we picked up on where Danny was goin' with it...

"I said, INDIANS!"

"YEAH!"

"INDIANS OF THE WILD MAGNOLIA COUNTREEE!!"

"YEAH!"

"COME NAH BRING THOSE INDIAN BLUES!"

"YEAH!"

"WITH UPTOWN SINGIN' AND DOWNTOWN TOONS!"

"YEAH!"

"WE SAYIN' HAHNDIE HAHNDIE AND A HAH NAH, NAY"

"HAHNDIE HAHNDIE YO' MAMA!

"WE GOT THE BLOODHOUNDS SWINGIN' FROM 'ROUND MY A WAY!"

"HAHNDIE HAHNDIE YO' MAMA!"

"AN' THOUGH WE GOT SO FAR, SO FAR YET TO GO!"

"HAHNDIE HAHNDIE YO' MAMA!"

"WE GONNA MARCH ON FOUR-MILES-A-MO-O-O!
"HAHNDIE HAHNDIE YO' MAMA!"

"AH SAY AHHHHH... AH NA NAY..."

"HAHNDIE HAHNDIE YO' MAMA!"

"AH SAY AHHHHH... AH NA NAY..."

"HAHNDIE HAHNDIE YO' MAMA!"

We stopped marchin' altogether, and started "buck jumpin" like a "second line," down that ol' access road, in the summer sun.

Now, buck jumpin' was fine when you could go inside, sit down, and drink a coke when ya' got tired. But it was another thing entirely when you was out in the middle-a-nowhere in 98 degree heat...and we really hadn't hiked that much during the school year. Big Ed, Jr. was the first to stop.

"Man, I'm gettin' tired... Can we stop and rest, Johnny?"

"Not yet, Ed...we gotta make time..."

"Make time for what, Johnny" said Auston, "I'm gettin tired too..."

"...and thirsty," said Will.

"Thirsty? Didn't you bring enough water?"

"I... I just don't know, man..."

"C'mon Johnny," said Danny, "let's stop... just for a couple-a-minutes..."

"Well... okay let's stop..."

"Whew!" said Ed. "I never thought we'd stop, man, I'm tired..."

Big Ed, Jr. sat down against the guardrail, resting his back against an old sign.

"Johnny, when we gonna get to the marsh?"

Ed leaned back, stretching his arms to yawn, fell backward over the guardrail and broke the sign. We busted out laughin' at first...then we felt kinda bad for him and went to help him up. Mark got to him first, and noticed the ol' dirty sign he broke read...

St. Christopher's Marsh...

"HEY! WE'RE HERE!"

Everybody else ran over to where Ed, Mark, and the sign were. Mark took out the riddle from the map while I took out the map again, with my compass.

"Awright Bloodhounds, We've made it this far. It's hot, and I know some of us are tired... But we gotta get a move on... We probably got at least 3 or 4 more miles to hike into this marsh before we get to where the money might be hid...we don't know what else might be out here b'sides us and..."

"B'sides us?" Said Ed. "...what'chu mean, b'sides us?!"

"What else is out here, Johnny?"

They were soundin' a lil' scared...so I had to come up with somethin' sensible...

"Well... I mean... This is a marsh, right? Well...there's gotta be stuff like alligators..."

"ALLIGATORS?!" yelled Ed.

"Yeah... and quicksand, and mosquitos, and you know..."

"Snakes..."

"...well, yeah I guess that too..."

"...and we have, what...FLASHLIGHTS?!"

"Auston," I said, "we'll make it..."

"Johnny, do we know where we're goin' yet?"

"Yeah Danny, we're goin' in there."

I pointed over Big Ed, Jr.'s shoulder, into the marsh.

"...anybody got a knife or somethin'?" said Auston.

Big Ed was less enthusiastic.

"...anybody got some bus fare, I'm outta..."

"C'mon fellas!" Mark said, "...stop whinin'! We're here; we made it this far...Lets finish it... Let's go get that money!"

Marshes in Louisiana were like people...kinda the same, but with real different personalities so they weren't all exactly alike. Some marshes were more shallow, and you could walk all right if you were careful. You might find yourself wadein' a bit, or you might even find some patches of "solid" ground. Other marshes, you wouldn't dare go in without a marsh buggy — a small boat with a gigantic fan attached to its back. The powerful motor and fan drove the boat by pushing the air behind it. We'd never been in a marsh before and so we were movin' strictly by faith — anything could happen to us...even drowning or bein' snake-bit, or worse...

But I had that same vision in my head of Mr. Willie and Ms. Verna and the store. And I wasn't alone. I knew Mark and the rest of the Bloodhounds had the same vision. So, no matter what happened, doin' this for them was worth it. What did them ol' folks say?

"Love will make a man do some crazy things…"

So Mark crossed over the guard rail and started walkin' into the marsh, and I wasn't far behind. Danny was next to go in, then Will, then Big Ed, Jr. leavin' Auston alone on the roadside. It didn't take much thinkin' over before Auston dug down deep, jumped the guard rail, and ran into the marsh after us.

It'd been hours since we entered St. Christopher's marsh. Evenin' was settin' in and The Bloodhounds were tired, worn, and beginning to lose faith. Big Ed kept sayin',

"…man, let's stop, my feet hurt, hunh…"

Auston kind'a lagged behind with Ed, but me and Mark and Danny and Will kept pace up front… Mark was good with maps and I learned how to use the compass from boy scouts, so we were doin' fine, until we got lost…

…the first time we got lost…
"Does anybody know WHERE WE ARE," said Big Ed, Jr.

"Sure," said Auston,

"We're in ST. CHRISTOPHER'S MARSH, stupid!"

"Man, this is crazy," Will said, "... how far off the highways are we?"

"I dunno Will, what'chu think?"

"YOU KNOW I don't know... Johnny?"

I checked the compass...

"We're headin' north..."

"Isn't that what you said AN HOUR AGO?!" exclaimed Ed.

"Yeah," Mark re-checked' the map, "... that's what he said, 'cuz that's what the map says, SO SHUT UP... we go north..."

Two hours later...we were still lost...

The guys started gettin' edgy. To be honest, we'd never done a night hike without adults leadin' the way, or supportin' us while we used our maps, compasses, and the night sky. With nightfall came the need for flashlights and more patience. We had some of one, and were almost out of the other.

"How long we got on these batteries, guys?"

"I dunno, we got these from Schwegmann's..."

SLAP!!

"...these mosquitos are big as horseflies..." cried Auston.

"Y'all said we goin north," said Big Ed, Jr. "...why this looks EXACTLY like the spot we were in ONE HOUR AGO?!

"Are we walkin' in circles, Danny?"

"I think so..."

"Johnny, you sure you got that compass right?"

"Mark, 'you sure you got the map right?!"

"Man, c'mon it's not like that..."

"Johnny," said Ed reachin' toward me, "lemme see the compass..."

"NO! Man you can't read no compass..." Then Auston jumped in it.

"You ain't doin' so good yourself podnuh..."

"Awright Ed, Auston, AND Johnny, y'all
STOP IT!" yelled Mark.

But they ignored Mark and jumped at me, so I
pulled back away from 'em both. They kept
grabbin' at me and me pullin' away caused the
compass to go airborne...

You ever played in a football game and
watched your worst nightmare come true, when
the other guy beats you on the pass, and there
ain't nothin' you could do about it? Or maybe
you dropped your mom's favorite crystal
punchbowl, after you kept tellin' her, I got it
mama"? It all goes by in slow motion... nothin'
you can do...

But watch...

That compass bounced three times on the ground.
...nobody could get to it...and...it fell in a pool of
quicksand... That thing sank like a lead brick.

"I TOLD Y'ALL TO STOP IT!" said Mark.

"Man that was stupid..." I said.

"Who you callin' stupid?" said Auston, "I ain't the one who's supposed to know how to use a compass..."

"Watch it, Auston..."

Mark was try'na defend me again, but I had it this time. I was so tired of Auston and his whinin' and complainin' and always thinkin' HE could do a better job than anyone else. So I got right in his face.

"So, you think you could'a done better?"

"Better than you..."

Mark jumped in between us and in the process, pushed Auston on the ground.

"STOP IT!

 Auston sat on the ground, probably shocked that Mark knocked him down so easily. Mark, red-faced and frustrated...let him have it...

"Now you know good and well that Johnny is the ONLY ONE who really learned how to use that thing...and now it's gone..."

"Yeah Aus,"Will added, "...you ain't got a badge..."

"BADGE?! WHAT I NEED A BADGE FOR?!"

Danny chimed in.

"Auston, you need t'shut up man... You know you couldn't read no compass..."

"Well this is just great, Bloodhounds... Whadda we do now?!" Ed said. "...we're lost, no compass, no trail, not even bread crumbs! I wanna go home..."

Ed was sayin' what I think was on everybody's minds. We'd lost the compass, it was gettin' later by the minute, we were lost in the middle a' nowhere, and we weren't any closer to findin' the money. We stopped, put our packs down, and started sittin' leanin' against trees, thinkin' about everything that had happened. Even though we'd lost the compass, we still had the map, and the riddle.

The map *and* **the riddle**...

So I got up and went over to Mark.

"What have we already done?"

"We've gone four Miles more north from Water's edge, turned left at yonder oak... 100 paces onward and, remember not to choke..."

While Mark continued to read, Big Ed, Jr. sat down on the end of an ol' dead tree.

"...your silent guide in moss is clad, His finger points the way..."

"AAAAGGGGHHH!!!!"

Just then that ol' dead tree Big Ed, Jr. was sittin' on crumbled under his weight, but there was somethin' stuck inside the tree. I put up my flashlight to where Ed had fallen and under him was.

A dead body...

"AAAAGGGGHHH!!!"

He crab-walked over to where the rest of us were... We were grabbin' onto each other like some scene outta Scooby -Doo!

After the initial shock of it... I got up the nerve to start walkin' toward the body. Ed tried to grab me.

"JOHNNY!

I was on the move...slowly... I shined the dim light upon the corpse, now covered in moss. The hand was stuck straight out, like somebody fell asleep that way. He had a ring on this finger, and was wearin' what looked like an old uniform.

The rest of the Bloodhounds moved in behind me.

"It's a... skeleton..."

"He looks nasty...," said Auston.

"And how is he SUPPOSED to look...he's DEAD! Mark said.

"Will, I ain't never seen a dead body before..."

"Me neither, Danny..."

"I seen dead," admitted Auston. "... You know cats and dogs and stuff..."

"Like when they get hit by a car or somethin'... but I ain't never seen one like this..."

I picked up a tree branch and reached toward the body.

"MAN, WHAT'CHU DOIN?!

"...try'na see what kind'a clothes he's wearin'..."

"...what, you goin' find his tailor?"

Stephen Alfred

I looked at Big Ed, Jr. Like he was crazy or somethin'...

"WHAT?!"

I used the branch to pull off some of the moss from the body. Then, I started to scan the body with the flashlight. There were old, tattered shreds of material stuck to the body, that I kept scrapein' at it 'til I could free it from the side of the corpse.

"It's a patch..."

"What does it say, Johnny?" said Danny.

"It says... "Braniff."

"It's a security company?"

"No, it's an armored car company..."

Mark and I were already on the same page.

"Ya' think..."

"Yeah Mark, I do..."

"Hey look!" said Will, "...his hand is up, and he looks like he's"

Pointing...

"Heeyyyy!" Mark yelled, "...your silent guide in moss is clad, His finger points the way..."

WE FOUND A CLUE — our biggest clue so far! So we gathered our things as Mark continued to read the riddle and we moved on.

"Which way is it pointin' Johnny?

I remembered when my daddy and my uncle Stan used to take me fishin' out by the gulf... They said you could find true north by lookin' at the stars...Ed didn't get what I was lookin' for.

"What'chu' lookin at, Johnny?

"Answer him, man what are you..."

"SHHH…" said Mark, "…shut up, Aus..."

"That way..."

"What, Johnny?" said Will.

"True north... He's pointing true north..."

With every step, I got more confident, more self-assured. We were gonna find that money! So I went back to Mark.

"What's the next part of the riddle?"

Mark picked his pen flashlight from his belt and studied the map and his notes from the riddle carefully.

"...and to two more like him just as bad have even less to say..."

"**Two** more *like him*?" said Auston. "You mean there's..."

"Yeah... Two more bodies... Let's keep movin'..."

Big Ed, Jr. was not likin' this part of the trip.

"I don't know 'bout y'all, but I'm about tired a seein' dead folk... My cousin-n-'em, they had a funeral parlor uptown... And my daddy used to take me by there when he needed to pick up somethin' from my uncle...they used to be fixin' up 'dem bodies in one room, and eatin' lunch in the next room...shoot, I couldn't never keep a appetite 'round stuff like that..."

"Ed?"

"What, Danny?"

"**Shut up, Ed...**"

We came into a clearing. The Spanish Moss-covered trees formed a type of canopy, like a natural tent… almost entirely blocking out the light of the moon. In the distance, there was a run-down shack, almost the size of a garage, set on tree stumps at the rear edge of the clearing. We started to run towards it, the riddle dancin' in my mind, and our flashlight beams bouncin' wildly across the clearing.

"Look!"

"Who'da thought this would be sittin' in the middle of this marsh?" exclaimed Mark.

"C'mon," I said, "… let's see what's inside…"

The Bloodhounds entered the shack cautiously. A single flashlight beam cut through the darkness… Then two, then three, until all of our lights filled the room.

"It's dark in here, even with the flashlights…"

"Anybody see a light switch?"

"Uh, Will… 'you see any power lines from NOPSI goin to this place?" said Auston.

"Oh…yeah… Never mind…"

Then, Auston's flashlight went out.

"My light's out!"

177

"Take mine," said Ed.

"NO, take mine..."

Danny gave Auston his flashlight.

"Thanks man... But what'chu gonna use?"

"I'm awright, I thought I saw an ol' oil lamp over in the corner."

"Be careful Danny..."

"Sure..."

Danny felt around in the darkness for a lamp, and found it on a table. As he tried to pick it up from the table, somethin' was pullin' at it from the other side. He probably thought it was just stuck on somethin' so he found the glass and raised it up to light it.

" AAAAAHHHHHGGGG!"

Danny started lookin' at Big Ed, Jr., who was, like stuck in a corner of the shack, pointin' and jumpin' up and down.

"What, Ed? What's wrong witchu'?"

By now, we all had our lights on Danny, so we could see it too...

178

"Ha…haaaaa...HAND!!!"

A bony hand and forearm still gripped the other side of the lamp.

Now we were all in the corner! Danny snatched his flashlight from back from Auston and started beatin' the side of the lamp, talkin' to it as he beat it, like his mama did when she whipped 'em.

"AAAAAHHHHHGGGG! I-DON'T-LIKE-NO- DEAD-BODIES HANGIN'-ON-ME-I-DON'T- LIKE IT- DON'T-LIKE IT!-DON'T-LIKE IT!"

The hand and forearm fell to the floor. Danny stood there, pantin', wheezin', and pointin' the flashlight toward the table where he got the lamp.

"LOOK!"

At the table, just sittin' there, were two more skeletons, wearin' armored car uniforms – almost completely intact. Mark read the last of the riddle.

"...but when you've found the last of them, while mute yet still they speak...their final gesture leads the way..."

"...to all that which you seek... "

"Johnny," said Ed, "what's a 'gesture' again?"

"Like…shootin' the bird at somebody or wavin' your hand…"

"Oh… I knew that…"

"Gesture?" said Auston, "I don't see nuthin' else."

"Mark, you see what they could be pointin' at?"

When Mark moved closer toward the table, I followed. We started studyin' the area for more clues. Mark put the light on one of 'em.

"Hey look… This one's got a clean hole, right in the head…"

"You mean he got…"

"Shot… Yeah…"

The other skeleton was slumped onto the table. I pulled it up, slow-like, by the shoulder, to sit it upright. Roaches started to run out from inside of the uniform, especially from a hole in the chest

"Uuhhh… that's nasty…"

"That's a whole," I said, "… a big one too…"

"So Johnny," said Auston, "…they both been shot?"

"Anybody been doin' the math?" asked Big Ed, Jr. "…this makes *three* dead bodies y'all… THREE… Now, I like the idea of the money and all, but I REALLY think we need to be leavin' this place, yeah…"

I understood his position, but we weren't about to come this far and leave empty-handed.

"You right, Ed…but we gotta get what we came for…their final gesture leads the way to all that which you seek…"

Mark noticed somethin' that slipped past the rest of us, even me.

"These bodies look like they been set up this way on purpose…"

I started trackin' the floor now, and noticed 6 or 7 of what looks pieces of old shredded newspaper on the floor. I bent down to pick 'em up.

"This is… MONEY!"

"What?" said Mark.

I put the light on three of 'em…tattered, worn, 100 dollar bills!

"Whoa," said Ed, "... This...this is one, two, THREE HUNDRED DOLLARS!

"There's more!"

Will picked up where I left off, searching the floor for more money. The trail of dollars led to a closet in the corner of the room. He tried to open the door, but it was stuck solid.

"I... Can't...open it..."

We all ran up to try to help him pull the door, Mark pryin' the door back, with an old metal pipe he's found on the floor. The door slowly pulled back, and busted off the hinges as we went flyin' to the floor. When we got up, we saw the ol' closet, filled, with twenty old, mildewed, canvas bags with WHITNEY NATIONAL BANK printed on them. The bags were almost filled the brim with money.

"THE MONEY!" Mark cried, "THIS IS IT!"

"WE FOUND IT!"

"WE FOUND IT?!"

WE WENT WILD!!! We were jumpin' around, dancin' with each other, grabbin' 20's and 50's and 100 dollar bills and throwin' 'em at each other by the fist-full!

After a while, we calmed down and started to pull the moneybags out into the middle of the floor, to pack our backpacks. We went from pandemonium to mute silence in a few minutes. Then, Big Ed spoke up.

"How much you think we got here, Mark?"

"I dunno, Ed— a whole lot..."

"That man at Madame Muvalla's said millions," I said.

"Millions?!"

Then Danny hit us with it.

"That means we... we're MILLIONAIRES?!"

"Yeah," said Ed, "... WE MILLIONAIRES...

I had to bring everybody back to earth for a minute.

"Whoa' na'... Y'all remember, the first thing we need to do with this money is help Mr. Willie and Miss Verna..."

Mark backed me up on this.

"He's right...that's what we promised..."

"Yeah, I know... But this is a whole lotta money y'all..."

"It is Aus, but first things first. We gotta pack all this up, get back home, and get this money to Miss Verna."

"It's late y'all..."

"Yeah what we gonna do?" said Ed, "...my daddy is gonna KILL me if we ain't back soon."

We finished packin' what we could carry...it was 15 million dollars, which, by my estimate meant each bloodhound would have ta' carry about 52 pounds each!

We were gonna have ta' leave some of it...

"What we gonna do with the rest of the money, Johnny?"

"Like I said, we'll come back for it later."

"You think we can do this again?"

"Sure," Mark interjected, "... Next time it'll be a lot easier."

"Maybe we should tell our folks...ya' know, they could help us..."

"Ed, they'll just take the money...stupid..."

"Say you Auston, who you callin' stupid?!

"Awright y'all stop it!" said Mark, "...Auston would you just shut up with that!"

But Big Ed, Jr. was right...I mean, after we helped Mr. Willie and Miss Verna and all... maybe we *should* tell our folks... They'd really know what to do with the money...

"They gonna turn it in, to the police" Auston protested, "...we ain't gonna be able to do nuthin' with it then..."

Ed was still right though...

"Well, maybe so, but maybe not... We can let them decide... besides, we're 12 years old. What are we gonna look like, try'na walk around with a few million dollars?"

"He's right, Aus..." Ed added.

"Yeah... well...I guess so..."

Will was lookin' at the sky...worried.

"It's gotta be real late y'all."

"We still got some time, don't we, Mark?"

185

Mark put his flashlight up to his watch.

"We don't have much time..."

"YOU GOT THAT RIGHT LIL' MAN..."

The air was frozen, and the only sound that could float on it was the gruff, deep, growlin' voice of some man who came outta nowhere. He was kinda tall, lanky, just standin' there with a flashlight in one hand.

And a long knife in the other...

"...and who are YOU?" said Auston.

"The name's Morris... Julius Montgomery Morris III. And that's *my money* you got in them bags..."

CHAPTER 7

We were in total shock... here it was, the man who must've done all a' this, was standin' right in front of us. He looked like a real killer too, even in dim light. I was scared — I guess we all were. I couldn't believe we'd gotten this far, just for this man to come in and take it all from us... He could kill us all. But there are times when even fear of bein' hurt or bein' killed won't stop you when you know your purpose. The Bloodhounds were supposed to bring that money back for Mr. Willie and Ms. Verna. This was what we *believed*. Nothin'...not even a man with a knife was gonna stop us...so I spoke up...

"How...How you gonna say it's *your* money?"

"Cuz I'm the one who put it out here..."

"YOU put it out here?" said Mark.

Morris moved in closer.

"Yeah son, *I PUT IT OUT HERE...* I think some congratulations are in order, I mean... I never would 'a thought some lil' punks like you would be able to come all this way and find *my* money... Hell, I almost forgot where I put it, bein' this marsh is so big and all...

But I see why they call y'all Bloodhounds... Y'all tracked my money down like you got a scent for it, that's good, yeah...who figured out my riddle?

Everybody else pointed to Mark and me — like as if they were gonna get punished or somethin'. Morris looked at both of us, and a huge grin grew on his twisted face. He started bein' a lil' condescendin' to us...

"Hey, good job, good job... A lot a grown folk's wouldn'a figured it out... Grown folks don't figure out a lotta things...Like them two in there, and the other one...they thought *they* was so smart..."

Then, Morris took us all back, tellin' the rest of the story.

"Jack, one of the armored car boys...that was the one who thought he was the mastermind or somethin'...he used to deliver to the bank for years. 'Guess he got tired of an armored car guard's pay... Anyway, he gets a guy I did time

with, Mason, to go in on an idea to hit the
Whitney. "Til then, nobody ever robbed the place,
not especially in broad daylight...

We met in Mason's kitchen and he tells me,
they needed somebody that NOBODY would
suspect to help put this job together. They needed
somebody who knew the schedule inside the
bank, the personnel, the whole thing...

I was workin' as a clean-up man in the place,
so I knew it all. I could give 'em dates, times,
anything they needed... So, I wanted in... all the
way in...So, I tell 'em what I know about the
place, how easy it's gonna be, and how many men
we needed to do it right... Jack...he always
thought he was so smart, he tries to argue with
me about what goes down in the bank... He ain't
even in the place for more than 25 or 30 minutes
on any day, while I work there 45-60 hours a
week! Anyway, Jack tries to convince Mason they
don't need me, AFTER I give 'em the info they
need. Mason almost falls for it, 'til I tell 'em I
know just as many cops as I know hoods... So, he
backs down...better to get the money and give me
my take, than to botch the whole thing and end
up back in prison...

So, we met up at the warehouse, got all the
other personnel, and laid out the final plan. Some
a' dem white boys didn't like the idea of a spook
bein' in on the job and havin' to split the money

with 'em. But it was my plan, and it was a good plan. I devised it, 'cuz I knew how everything worked there. I might'a been emptyin' trash and moppin' floors, but I was like a fly on the wall. I caught everything 'dem white folks did every day. So I knew how to make it happen. Everybody had to be in place to make it work. And everybody who had anything to do with the bank, the guards, and me...we needed to continue to come to work every day for a while after the job, so as not to 'rouse suspicion...

When it was time to do the job, everything went off without a hitch. The guards inside the bank were totally caught with their pants down. I played innocent bystander like a pro. The tellers filled up the bags...If everybody wasn't so scared, they probably would 'a wondered, "what 'dem guard's smilin' about...we gettin' robbed!" But the joke was on them...nobody was the wiser...

The Armored car boys and I met the three robbers at the old warehouse—they'd been celebratin'. All around 'em were stacks of 20's, 50's and 100 dollar bills, money bands and bags. It was kind of a shame we had ta'cut their celebration short...

So, after we killed 'em, I watched the boys pack the money back into the bags. Jack, the know-it-all, seemed a lil' steamed that I wasn't packin' right along with 'em. I can remember 'im

sayin' "Say spook, what…you too good to pack
up this money now?" I gave 'im my "step-n-fetch-
it" routine. "Naw missuh Jack suh, Ahs jus,
watchin' for duh heat…"

The plan was, to take the money out to the
wood shack, and let it stay there for a while, 'til
thing's cooled off… I used to overhear the bank
manager talk about other banks gettin' hit, and
how he'd say, "they're covered by insurance" so;
the customers would get the money back anyway.
So, it wasn't like as if the people would really
miss anything… We'd get paid, the people would
get their money back from insurance on the bank,
ev'rybody wins…

But when we got to the clearin' by the shack,
Jack decided he had other plans… he told me,

"Awright, Morris, end-a-the line…drop da
piece…"

He's got the drop on me. You could tell he
was thinkin' a' this in his lil' twisted mind for a
minute. He didn't like no black folks, 'specially
smart ones, like me. He had no intention of
splittin' that money with a spook… But what he
didn't know was, I had other plans too… I
remember 'im sayin' somethin' like…

"..You know we can't leave him alive after all this...I mean, think about it, who do you think is gonna be lookin' for a jig like you, out here?"

"I remember him havin' a whole lotta mouth..."You gonna shoot me, or talk me to death?"

"I remember the last thing that ol'fay said to me..."

"Oh... You got jokes? A funny dead man? ...Well laugh at this Ni-"

"BLAM! BLAM!

I got 'im before he could get the '-ger' out—him, and his boy, Mike...Doug I really felt sorry for...poor schmuck, never knew how deep he was in...too deep to crawl out...He begged me,"

"Please... Please don't kill me... I like you people... Nobody's gonna find out I swear..." So I walked right up to 'im, and I assured 'im

"You know somethin'... You right..."

"I gutted 'im like a fish on a Friday..."

I couldn't move...We couldn't move... Morris had a gun in one hand, a lamp in the other. Now that we knew exactly what he did and how... he was scarier than ever.

"So, Nobody found out...'til now..."

"Now hold on mister," said Ed, "...you ain't thinkin' a doin' somethin' to us kids are you?! I mean, there's laws and... and stuff like that..."

"SHUT UP ED!" Auston snapped.

Ed still pled his case...OUR case..."

"Wha... Why you left the money out here for so long? You forgot about it or somethin'?"

"NO... a few weeks after the bank job, I got pinched on another charge... I kind 'a...shot somebody... But, since he was jus' some low-life folks didn't care about, I only got 15 years...I served a lil' over ten..."

"So, what'chu gonna do with us mistuh," said Will.

"Y'all been good boys up to now, I just wanna get my money, and I'll let you go 'bout ya bizness..."

"Jus' like that... You'll let us go?!"

"No Ed," said Danny, "... He ain't try'na let us get outta here alive, stupid..."

"WHAT?!"

Danny was right... Morris had no intention of lettin' six 12 and 13 year-olds get in the way of 15 million dollars.

"I promise," said Morris, "...'won't do you like I did them other guys... I'll have ta' kill ya' quick...so you don't suffer too much..."

"HEY MISTER!" said Auston, "...you can't cut us all! You got one knife and there's six of us!"

I Could See His Point...

"Yeah," said Danny, "...c'mon Bloodhounds... He can't take all of us!"

"Oh yeah," said Morris, "...ya' got a good point..."

Morris dropped the knife. You could hear one big sigh of relief...that is, 'til he pulled out his pistol...

"HE GOT A GUN Y'ALL!!!"

"Boys...this revolver got *six* bullets..."

He pointed the long, silver barrel at each of us, accentuatin' his words while he pointed it at us.

"One-for- each-one-a'-you..."

"You ain't that fast, mistuh" said Mark.

I wish Mark hadn'a said that...

"YOU WANNA FIND OUT BOY?! I' been waitin' over 10 years for my money, and I want it...NOW...I gotta give it to ya'... Y'all some real good bloodhounds... But, even bloodhounds, gotta be put down, when they've outlived their purpose...

He got us all outside with the money in our packs, plus the other money we couldn't fit in there. The walk seemed to take forever...My mind was racin' thinkin' about Mr. Willie, Ms. Verna...my mama...my daddy...

And my boys...

I kept tryna think of what I could do, what we could do to get away from him. Morris was crazy and a real killer, not some comic book bad-guy, or some made up bedtime story...he was real...

For a minute, my mind wandered when I smelled the odor of the marsh in the night summer breeze. Up to then, the heat blanketed the marsh like it would suffocate us all. So, that breeze comin' in was like a breath of fresh air...

I knew what was gonna happen and I couldn't let it go that way...I had only one card left to play...so I played it..."Mistuh Morris?"

"What?"

"We can't give you this money."

His smug grin sunk into this real, twisted-up, look on his face, like somebody sat on his head and fotted.

"WHAT?!"

"It's not ours to give you... 'See, we came out here to get this money for some people who need it... People we love... Bloodhounds are loyal, and strong, and fearless, didn't you know that, Mistuh Morris? You got a gun, but we got each other...an' that's stronger than any bullets you say you got for us...

It might 'a been kinda corny, but it was true. Auston, Mark, and Big Ed, Jr. spoke up, one behind the other.

"Yeah, Mistuh... Don't you know?
"Haven't you heard?"

"We the Bloodhounds!

"AND BLOODHOUNDS FROM BACK-A-TOWN DON'T BACK DOWN!"

Without sayin' a word to each other, we all came to the same conclusion...we were not gonna die that night...

Morris raised the pistol, pointing it straight at me. I wasn't scared, I just knew he couldn't do it. All of a sudden,

BLAM! BLAM!

Morris' hand flew up in the air as the shots rang out. He hit the ground hollerin' and as we put our flashlights on him, we knew exactly why.

"POOCHIEEEE!!!"

THAT DOG!! Poochie had to have followed that bus, and followed us... ALL THE WAY TO THE MARSH! He jumped at MORRIS' right arm, just in time, knockin' him and the pistol on the ground. And just like the compass, that pistol bounced, and fell into a pool of quicksand!

Now *we* had the advantage...

"BLOODHOUNDS! ...CAPTURE THE FLAG, NOW!"

197

"AAAAHHHHHHGGG!"

The Bloodhounds ran in all directions through the Marsh. When we played "capture the flag" on our scoutin' trips, we had a strategy to scatter in all directions and evade capture by other troops. Even though this was a marsh, it wasn't too different from Scout's Island, where we always camped. We might not've known how to fight a grown man with a knife, but what we did know was how to hide.

Morris scrambled around lookin' for the lamp, and for his pistol. Surprisingly, the lamp wasn't broken, and while the gun was gone, he did find his knife. Since he knew we had the advantage, the only thing he could do was try head-games...

"WHERE YA' AT?! YA' KNOW I'M GONNA KILL EVERY LAST ONE OF YA' WHEN I FIND YA! YA' AIN'T GETTIN' OUT THIS MARSH ALIVE!!!"

Mark and me maneuvered around a large tree and watched 'im walk past. Ya' could see he was trailin' the money, 100 dollar bills, scattered around the ground.

"YOU DROPPIN' MY MONEY ALL OVER THIS MARSH!"

You could hear him mumblin' to himself, "I gotta kill 'em... They wastin' my money..."

Danny and Will were hidden behind another tree. Poochie was with 'em, beginning to growl, when Will covered his muzzle.

"Stop, Poochie! Quiet!"

Big Ed, Jr. and Auston were hidden behind the rear of the wood shack, near an old marsh buggy.

"Aus, I'm scared..."

"Shut up, Ed... I am too..."

"I'M GONNA FIND YOU, AND WHEN I DO..."

Morris kept lookin' at the ground and he found Danny and Will's footprints. He tracked 'em 'til he could see Poochie's tail just on the other side of the tree.

"I GOT YOU NOW!"

Danny and Will were pinned against the tree by Morris on one side, and by a pool of quicksand on the other. Poochie wheeled around to face Morris growling...

"Nice Doggie..."

Poochie leaped into the air at Morris…you could see him swing, then the dog cried out and fell on the ground. I could hear Will screamin'

"POOCHIEEE!"

Morris started to mock 'im.

"POOCHIE!" STOP IT BOY! HE'S JUST A MUTT… 'AIN'T EVEN A BLOODHOUND!"

Will and Danny crowded together against the tree, as Morris moved in for the kill. He lifted up his knife, and was about to come down with it when…

BAMM!

Outta nowhere, a tree limb hit Morris in the head! Will cried out,

"COO-CORN BREAD?!!!"

It was Coo-Corn Bread! He hit Morris with a big ol' tree limb, and down Morris went, right on top of the lantern!

"AAAAAHHHHHGGGG!!!" Morris cried.

The lamp had broke open under him and the kerosene and flame lit him up like an Ascension Parish Bonfire at Christmas!

He ended up runnin' through the marsh, past Danny and Will try'na to put the flames out...

I guess nobody ever taught'im "stop-drop-n-roll..."

He dove in some water...then found out it wasn't water at all.

"HELP ME! HELP ME! DON'T LET ME DIE! DON'T LET ME..."

By some miracle, we all managed to stay outta the quicksand. There were pools of it all over the marshlands. But Morris wasn't so lucky... For a minute, it looked like Danny and Will were 'bout to move to save 'im, but the pull a' that stuff was too fast. Grown folks used to tell us that the more you fought it, the faster you sank...They were right...it *killed'im quick*...

I stood at the edge of the quicksand, wonderin' if he would come back up, like somethin' from "creature from the black lagoon."

"He ain't comin' back up Johnny..."

Coo-Corn Bread was behind me, with Danny, Will, and the rest of the Bloodhounds. Here was this man, Coo-Corn Bread...who some people made fun of and others called crazy...a man who didn't have much of anything…this man saved our lives.

And saved our dream…

"How did you find us?" I asked. Coo-Corn Bread stopped.

"…same way the dog did, I followed you… I knew the only way you'd be leavin' Hardin on its biggest day, gettin' on the Broad bus with backpacks, and headin' toward the east was if you found that map and you was goin' to St. Christopher's. I figured you'd need more than jus' ol' Poochie if ya' got in a pinch…"

He tracked us… he cared enough for us, kids who were scared a'him… he cared about us…

"Coo-Corn Bread?"

"Yeah, son?"

"Thanks… Thanks for everything…" A big smile grew over Coo-Corn Bread's weary and worn face.

"Gla…Glad To help…"

In that moment, it hit me. No one ever thanked him for anything… he had served in the military, lost his mind while fightin' for his country, and people had all but thrown him away. 'Cept for a few folk in the neighborhood who would give him food, he really didn't have nobody. We all decided that night that he would always have the Bloodhounds.

We checked everybody out, and no one was hurt…'cept Poochie…

"He's… He's got a cut under his left side," Said Coo-Corn Bread.

Coo-Corn Bread ripped part of his shirt sleeve off, and tied it around the wound. Even though he was still whinin' now Poochie started waggin' his tail.

"He's gonna be awright boys."

"You…sure Coo-Corn Bread?" asked Will.

"Yeah…I'm sure…"

It was really late now. We had to get outta the marsh, back to the bus line, and home before anyone started askin' questions.

"Mark, what time is it?"

"Time for you to stop asking what time is it, Ed…"

"Why, Auston?"

"'Cuz you startin' to work on my nerves, yeah..."

"Johnny, how long you think it's gonna take us to get back?"

"I dunno, Danny... we walked around in circles for a couple of hours before we got to the clues... It don't look like..."

VRROOOOM! VRROOOM!!

We all jumped at the sound of an engine roaring. Coo-Corn Bread had started up a marsh buggy that was parked out behind the wood shack.

"Y'all comin'?"

"HEY! We got another way outta here!" said Will.

So we loaded up ALL OF THE MONEY...from our packs, and from the money bags, into the back of the buggy. Will carried Poochie, and put him real gently on the floor of the buggy.

For a minute there...I thought we might not make it out alive... 'Good thing Poochie had been followin' us since the bus stop... I'm sure glad that dog didn't like no chains. And even though he was a mutt, he was a true Bloodhound at heart...

We all took one, long look around at the shack, and the marsh, for one the last time. We were just twelve and thirteen year-olds, but it felt like we aged by 'bout ten years since we went out to St. Christopher's Marsh. The buggy slowly pulled out from the bank, turning for an opening to an outlet on the east side of the marsh.

We were goin' *home*...

EPILOGUE

We made it back home, and thanks to Coo-Corn Bread, made good on our promise. Mr. Willie and Miss Verna were NOT gonna lose their house, or their business. And ALL Mr. Willie's hospital bills were gonna get paid.

Most people would jus' walk by Coo-Corn Bread without sayin' a word, 'cuz ev'rybody used to say he was crazy. But THE LORD used him to save our lives that night. And he helped Mr. Willie — an old friend who always looked out for him, and who never judged him...

We had to pay Father Mike a visit too... We knew the Church and the School needed things, and we knew they didn't have the money they used to. So, we rang the doorbell at the rectory, and ran. When Father Mike came to the door, he found a lil' somethin' more than some prank on the welcome mat...

...They wouldn't have to have no mo' bingo...not for a while anyway...

And you know we had to pay The Greater Mt. Zion Baptist Church a visit as well... They were always doin' good things in Back-a-town and around the city, with little or no money...

Pastor and Sister Willborn found a "package" at the back door of the church with a note to let them know that now they could finally send those missionaries to Africa, and to South America, and officially change their name to, "The Greater Mt. Zion MISSIONARY Baptist Church!"

Our last stop was Hardin Park. They always got some of their uniforms and equipment stolen ev'ry year! Next season... it was gonna be different, I guarantee... In fact, now that we found the money, EVERYTHING was gonna be DIFFERENT...

Well...almost everything... Ya' see, I forgot to mention, we made it back home from St. Christopher's Marsh...late...What was worse, somebody told our folks they saw us at the Broad bus stop when we were supposed to be at Hardin Park!

That Larry Charbonnet!

When I say, "ev'rybody got their butt whipped," I mean, EV'RYBODY GOT THEIR BUTT WHIPPED! We were all grounded for a month. But it wasn't gonna change our outlook on things... We had changed, and with it, came the promise of new things...things we never would 'a thought possible before... like me goin' to see Marie AT HER NANAIN'S HOUSE...

After my punishment was up, I actually got up the nerve to walk up to Marie's Nanain and Parrain's house, to ask to "see" her! ME! I walked up the steps to the front door. Not scared... flowers and candy in my hand...

I rang the doorbell, and I waited...

...AND HER NANAIN SAID YES!!!

Marie Desvigne's Nanain answered the door with her usual sternness and I handed her the flowers! Her face turned from that stern, mean look she was good for, to a big, wide, bright smile. She disappeared inside for only a minute, and then the door popped open.

It was Marie...

Yeah... no mo' sneakin' into Wendy Marchand's yard...Things were definitely gonna be different around Back-a-town...

We were gonna show 'dem "poo-puts" from across-the-way who really had the whip... by at least three or four touchdowns...

We proved it to 'em, yeah. You can't jus' mess wit no Bloodhounds... And while I know they got bloodhounds everywhere...

Don't you know?...

Haven't you heard?...

We the Bloodhounds from Back-a-town...and...

BLOODOUHNDS FROM BACK-A-TOWN DON'T BACK DOWN!

Thank you for reading "The Bloodhounds" by Stephen R. Alfred. Please leave a review and don't forget to check out other titles at Printhousebooks.com.

PRINTHOUSE BOOKS
Read it, Enjoy it, Tell a friend.

VIP INK Publishing Group, Incorporated.
Atlanta, GA.

www.PrintHouseBooks.com

Stephen Alfred